MUSKOKA

ESSENTIAL PROSE SERIES 218

**Canada Council Conseil des Arts
for the Arts du Canada**

**ONTARIO ARTS COUNCIL
CONSEIL DES ARTS DE L'ONTARIO**

an Ontario government agency
un organisme du gouvernement de l'Ont

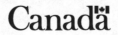

Guernica Editions Inc. acknowledges the support of the Canada Council
for the Arts and the Ontario Arts Council. The Ontario Arts Council
is an agency of the Government of Ontario.

We acknowledge the financial support of the Government of Canada.

MUSKOKA

JULIAN SAMUEL

**GUERNICA
EDITIONS**

TORONTO—CHICAGO—BUFFALO—LANCASTER (U.K.)

2024

Guernica Founder: Antonio D'Alfonso

Michael Mirolla, general editor
Michael Mirolla, editor
Interior and cover design: Errol F. Richardson

Guernica Editions Inc.
287 Templemead Drive, Hamilton, ON L8W 2W4
2250 Military Road, Tonawanda, N.Y. 14150-6000 U.S.A.
www.guernicaeditions.com

Distributors:
Independent Publishers Group (IPG)
600 North Pulaski Road, Chicago IL 60624
University of Toronto Press Distribution (UTP)
5201 Dufferin Street, Toronto (ON), Canada M3H 5T8

First edition.
Printed in Canada.

Legal Deposit—First Quarter
Library of Congress Catalog Card Number: 2023943449
Library and Archives Canada Cataloguing in Publication
Title: Muskoka / Julian Samuel.
Names: Samuel, Julian, author.
Series: Essential prose series ; 218.
Description: First edition. | Series statement: Essential prose series ; 218
Identifiers: Canadiana (print) 20230506623 | Canadiana (ebook) 2023050664X | ISBN
9781771838771
(softcover) | ISBN 9781771838788 (EPUB)
Subjects: LCGFT: Novels.
Classification: LCC PS8587.A3623 M87 2024 | DDC C813/.54—dc23

for Abouali Farmanfarmaian

Oh wearisome Condition of Humanity!
Borne under one Law, to another bound:
Vainely begot, and yet forbidden vanity,
Created sicke, commanded to be sound;
What meaneth Nature by these diverse Lawes?
Passion and reason, selfe-division cause.

—Faulke Greville

1. High School

I'm A SMALL-SCALE property manager who is good at dealing with people; however, my business partners find my innumeracy pitiful. I don't have any ability with numbers: moreover, I fear them. I still count on my fingers. I can't count in musical time either, but that's another matter. When we go looking for properties they like my overall assessment of a particular property and my sociological comprehension of the area. They laugh out loud at my calculations for mortgages, down payments, insurance, welcome taxes, and my conversions from square feet to square metres. Conversions are essential because we live in Canada.

In the recent past, myself and two business partners—I'll nickname them Zero and One—were at a restaurant in Toronto's Little Italy celebrating a successful sale of a mid-sized property, and right away we were contemplating reinvesting the profit in purchasing a fourteen unit building.

Zero takes a sip of wine and asks: "Mohammed, please figure out what we'd pay as a monthly mortgage if we put $200,000 to $300,000 down?" Before I can answer, One interrupts. "So you think the seller is asking way too much? Should we put more down or might we need some cash for repairs?"

Zero and One can see that I'm clueless.

"I haven't done the numbers yet," I say. On the restaurant table, I use One's laptop for online mortgage calculations and the small printing calculator. There is a nice glass of Amarone near my right hand. Sunlight flows through the wine and makes a bright patch on the table.

One and, to a lesser extent, Zero always think about getting more property right after a sale. Zero and One do all the thinking, I sheepishly follow and make some profit.

One looks at Zero, then at me and asks: "What might the monthly expenses be? Ballpark? Include monthly mortgage, and any other expenses in your estimate."

"Other expenses?"

"Yeah, electricity, insurance, property management, maintenance you know, just like last time," Zero says.

After a few minutes, I pass them my neatly written calculations. Zero and One put their shoulders together and look at my numbers. One says: "Mohammed, you've made a bunch of errors but overall I think you've learnt lots."

"Zero and One, you are great teachers. Income stream minus expenses."

Zero says: "Yeah, you're okay with that, but, Mohammed, the amortization figures are off the over-heating planet. I wonder what Paul Krugman would say about your figures? For the love of Christ, Mohammed, stay with us here on planet real-estate."

"Do you now know how to look up a property on MLS?" Zero asks.

"Well, not as well as you two, but at least I managed to get us all together to do another deal."

"Thanks for bringing us all together," One says. "You should manage our stock trading account. We'd really be flying then."

With my retirement clearly on the horizon, I've decided to go to adult high school to study grade 12 math and physics. Perhaps, I'll be less scared of numbers in the future. Back in the homeland, my grandfather was a geometer, and therefore was good at maths. Unfortunately, that epigenetic inheritance didn't follow me to Canada.

To get to Saint Mungo College, I take the southbound Bathurst bus to Bloor Station. On the subway people are wearing acrylic finger nails that are so long their fingers can't be curled around the holding poles. There isn't any connection between race and acrylic nail extensions. Every day, I look for the longest nails on either a man or a woman, and wonder how they clean their bums. What happens to the toilet paper with those incisive nails? Surely, these nails must fail spectacularly. On Monday, people have shorter acrylics than on Friday or the weekend. Or is this in my mind?

Saint Mungo College looks like it has experienced budget cuts since it was a blueprint. The toilet smells of colonial-period Dettol, a paper towel roller with its left side hinge broken hanging from the wall, empty holes where screws have fallen, soap splatters on the mirror, plaster powder on the floor, and toilet paper which is sub-atomically thin. One has to pinch one's nose while peeing. These urological details will be important to my story.

But first the guidance counsellor interviews me from behind a desk filled with stacks of papers.

"There is a 50-dollar fee."

"I'm living on a pension and can't afford to pay this."

"Okay, I'll ask the vice principal. Maybe the fee can be waived." She leaves the room and a few minutes later returns. "No problem about the fee."

She asks me about my educational background. "I have a BA in English Literature from Trent University and an MFA from Concordia in Photography."

"What languages do you speak?"

"English, French and Urdu." Being a Torontonian, she knows right away what Urdu is and continues filling out the online application.

"Okay, everything is set. Would you like to start today?"

"Yes, I would. Please, I have a question: Why would the school want proof of my citizenship?"

"This is a ministry requirement. I'm sorry about it, but I'm obligated to ask this question. Paul is your teacher, and we just use first names here. It was a pleasure to meet you, Mohammed."

I head to Paul's class. Standing in front of the class, the math teacher asks each of us why we are taking mathematics. He looks at me. I say: "I think maths is a way to understand how society works." The teacher blinks but otherwise doesn't alter his expression. Another student says: "I need my high-school diploma because I want to study interior design at George Brown College. I have my high-school education in Rangoon but that is not accepted here. So, I'm doing high school again."

There are eight of us in the class. Ayesha and Marium, both from Ethiopia, say that they need to pass this course to continue into higher education. Osman, from Mogadishu, repeats what they say. Chandri Chandrasekhar, whom I will come to sit beside every day, is a bright and friendly woman from Assam. Says she has two daughters who need help with their maths homework, and she herself is also interested in the subject. Leaning over, she whispers that she is not related to Subrahmanyan Chandrasekhar. I have no clue who he is. A quick look at my cellphone sitting on my lap shows me that he was born in Lahore and studied in Madras, England and America. In 1983, he and William Alfred Fowler shared the Nobel Prize for Physics.

Then it's Deana's turn to say something. Dressed in tight jeans, and a white shirt, she straightens her back and addresses the class in clear, region-less English:

"My name is Deana Nibaa-Niba'ar. I've worked in Human Resources right here in Toronto." She pauses as if she were about to make a long speech. "And I now want to catch up. I'm here to learn math and science. I appreciate being here. I am originally from the Forest Hills reserve in northern Ontario. I'm Indigenous in two ways: my mother is from Forest Hills Nation, my father is also from the Forest Hills Nation as well as from an ancient people in Peru. I've lived in Toronto most of my life … I can't speak my native language."

The confession falls flat on the mathematicians from Adidas Ababa. The teacher and the entire class feel at ease with her. Deana is admired. Her elegance indicates that she knows a better world than this run-down, underfunded, inner-city school.

The class clock comes up to 9. Every day at this time, the principal's voice crackles with reverence and solemnity through the speaker. I imagine him sitting in a cave in Jalalabad filled with empty Amazon Prime delivery boxes.

"Out of respect for Indigenous peoples in Canada, we acknowledge that all Toronto Catholic District School Board properties are situated on traditional territories. The territories include the Wendat, the Anishinabek (a-ni-shna-bek) Nation, the Haudenosaunee (hoh-Dee-noh-Shoh-nee) Confederacy, and the Mississaugas of the Credit First Nations. We also recognize the contributions and enduring presence of all First Nations, Métis, and Inuit people in Ontario and the rest of Canada. Please stand for O Canada."

I remain seated. Deana doesn't stand either. She has noticed that I am not standing. All the other students are up on their feet.

There are no Chinese students in class, yet. Andrew, who is a Filipino, has small scrunched handwriting that appears as though the numbers were squeezed in a merciless vice. He writes with a ballpoint pen, not a mechanical pencil like the rest of us.

O Canada our home and native land ...

Now native to Canada as the anthem proclaims. Chandri speaks enough Hindustani to chat with me in Urdu. The math problems written as word questions confuse her. The two Ethiopians side step their deficiency in English by resorting to pre-bibical Amharic to figure out the Pythagorean problems. Since early February I've been arriving early for my class which starts at 0915 and finishes at 1130. The teacher is always happy to see me. He and I chat about local and international politics. He wants to see cuts to welfare, wants Julian Assange sent to America to be put into solitary confinement for the rest of his life and more. On his desk I see a book by Jordan Peterson, a University of Toronto psychology professor who has achieved media popularity worldwide for his classical liberal position on equity-seeking groups and the forced use of non-specific pronouns.

I ask Paul: "What does Peterson think about everything?"

"I can't really say. If I say anything it might get to the principal and then what would happen to me?"

"Can they fire you for having views?"

Paul shrugs. His blackboard handwriting is beautiful and he's a great teacher.

A man from Chad will soon have to drop the course because he rarely comes to class and when he does he falls asleep. He has two jobs, he says. He couldn't work out how to calculate m in the the linear equation $y = mx + b$. After the blackboard demo by the teacher, Chad approaches me for help. I help him. "y is delta y over delta x—remember x is the independent variable." He nods, pretending to understand how to find slopes of x and y coordinates. Rise over run. Both Deana and I like glancing at super hot Leonor, the Argentine Toronto-born student to our left. Unlike me, Leonor can fit ten math problems on a single page. Her handwriting has ancient Harappa-era looking lilting 9s, compressed fat bottom 6s, balloonish 8s, and beyond oblate 0s that suggest mysterious tunnels leading to wormholes in the cosmos.

Deana doesn't sit beside me, but is nearby. She is friendly with me and has none of the typical South Asian social caution towards men.

We have listened through many renditions of *O Canada*. During the coffee break Deana tells me certain equations are indigenous to nature; we can see the mathematical regularities of flower stems and petals. She asks me what I think about *O Canada* and the native land acknowledgment.

"Deana, I think they are a waste of breath. Sending all these words daily from every single elementary and high school in Canada to the First Nations is meant to make middle-class settlers feel less guilty." I've used the word *settler* as ass-cover.

"Be patient, something good could come from it."

"Okay."

After sipping coffee on the stairs, we return to class. On the blackboard Paul has written:

$$8mx + 4px - 6m - 3p$$

"Mohammed, will you come up and solve this?" I can feel Deana's eyes on my back, therefore I use my best chalkpersonship to impress her. The bracket is easy to draw, then I make a masculine number 2 and an engineer's wide 4, and more expressive numerals with a touch of mysterious calligraphy. I can feel my writing affecting Deana.

$$= (8mx + 4px) + (-6m - 3p)$$
$$= 4x(2m + p) - 3(2m + p)$$
$$= (2m + p)(4x - 3)$$

"I think the answer in the book is incorrect," I say. He looks surprised. I say: "But, Paul, the answer in the text book says: $2(m + p)(4x - 3)$. It's incorrect."

"Yes, Mohammed, let me see." He lifts his eyebrows. I am confident that the textbook is wrong. So is Chandri whose head moves along her y axis with Bollywoodian agreement. I sit down and Paul walks up to the board to do the equation. He looks at the two of us. "I'll make a note of that. You're right. You're both right. Math text books are filled with typographical errors."

"Do you mean filled with errors these days or …?"

"All math and science books have tons of typos."

Maths is about developing confidence. Enjoying the momentary euphoria of our mathematical victory over the text book, I meekly ask: "Please, would you consider giving me an additional mark for finding an error in the text? Is it an unreasonable request?"

The class makes a sound like scurrying mice. The bell rings to the clutter of closing binders and chairs scraped back on the faded linoleum floor. Deana makes returning to class everyday magical.

2. Home work in the park

A MILD FEBRUARY congenially flows into a milder than usual March. This is the class after spring break when the weather will change abruptly and the first birds will return: Robins, Starlings, Crows, Woodpeckers. I'm sitting beside Chandri noticing her stamped handwriting: Her 7s are Anglo-Indian without the Euro cross bar at the middle of the upright line; her 1s resemble Army swords, her 3s are round and resemble an *Om* in the Hindi alphabet. Her 5s echo sigma.

He's now started us on maths problems that are no longer arithmetic but sometimes refer to things that aren't real. But mostly they are real, like area, volume, circle and curve. Many here want to go to George Brown College for trades courses so they need these basics.

Deana has spontaneously developed an understanding of numbers in every kind of relationship possible. I make an excuse to go to her desk about a binomial I just invented:

$$i(5 + 4x) \times (3 + 2x)$$

"Deana, maybe this is an indigenous equation and we can solve it by using Traditional Environmental Knowledge."

"Yes, that knowledge is high-tech. One day we should meet to do some homework." Wow, has she really suggested that we meet? I ask myself. "Yes, that's a good idea."

I am surprised by Deana's invitation. And my own eagerness to agree. Did I sound too willing? We return to class after the week-long break. Paul opens the windows because the classroom doesn't have its own thermostat.

Outside, birds are singing in the early March thaw. Nearby a male Robin is dueting with a male Robin. "I'm a vigorous male—

let's make Robins," it sings. "I'm a healthy male—let's make nests," sings the other. Somewhere close by a female Robin is listening, invisibly comparing suitors. The first bird sends a song across the school parking lot; its notes follow the parabolic:

$$y = -1/2x^{\wedge}(2)+6$$

The second sends a response song along the following path:

$$y = -1/4x^{\wedge}(2)+6$$

A cardinal high up in a tree to the right intercepts with: $x = 0$ and $y = 6$. There is no answering song. Puzzlingly, all the bird songs stop. This is due—and I am guessing here—to the superposition of an ambulance siren which collapses the wave functions of the bird songs. Deana and I believe this to be the case because we are taking grade 12 Mungo physics.

Robins dominate all the songs with the energy that comes from eating the free electrons that live in ground-state worms. A large black crow sits and observes the robins and, because he hears and observes, he shape-shifts into a robin. This change, according to Deana, would have happened even if we weren't present because the universe is filled with things that exist even if we are not there to observe them. Myriads of other thing-beings exchanging sensations are present, making each other more real. My emotional shape is changing the more time I spend near Deana.

The students in the mathematics course are from all over the Third World; they are happy they are no longer in war zones. The Syrians are the happiest, but many still cover their heads. How can that make them happy? They'd see that as a trivial question, I'm sure. Everyone comes from countries with governments that are brutal toward their own citizens, so understandably, they proudly stand up for O Canada, especially if sung by Ginette Reno dressed in a hijab. The teacher is sitting at the back playing with his mobile.

A few birds from Quebec have entered the equations. A Cardinal with the spirit of Leonard Cohen sits on a wire outside. The birds pour out wild polynomials, jamming the functions in our scientific calculators, but the equations ultimately come to rest on calm graph paper in our notebooks as solutions bearing feathers.

We are having the hottest spring thaw in decades. After class, Deana and I agree to meet at the Tichester entrance of the Cedervale ravine. I've arrived first, and watch her park her car and walk toward me. An hour-glass mass enjoying free forward momentum.

"Difficulty finding the park?" Deana often speaks in abbreviated tweet-like sentences. I try to imitate her.

"A nice bench underneath the trees. Saint Mungo was the patron saint of alcoholics?" We sit down and I open my notebook. I'm sure she has noticed me looking at her.

"Patron saint? How did he get to be that?"

"He's the patron saint of the city of Glasgow."

Deana eyes me suspiciously. I don't think she believes anything I say.

"Let's start with this one," she says pointing to the open page in my notebook.

With my zero point-nine pencil, I've written:

$$x^{2} + 4 - 4$$

I look at her. Deana expects me to finish writing the entire problem. I find myself looking at her constantly. We're under a blue evening sky with puffy pink clouds moving from west to east. Up there it must be windy but down here in Cedervale ravine near Tichester and Bathurst streets it's an almost warm late spring evening. I think to myself: What's going to happen now that I'm sitting beside her on this park bench? The friendship is moving beyond math. I rewrite the number and letter on the left-hand side of the page. Deana, assertively says: "Write the entire equation."

"Okay, I'll do it."

$$x^{(2)} + 4 - 4 = 0$$

"Yes, Mohammed, an equation needs an equal sign in it," she says as her hand accidentally brushes against mine. Then in a relaxed way she stops our homework and asks me what I like to eat. What parts of the city do I shop in? Do I like visiting the waterfront to see the tall ships? Do I like leaving the city? She doesn't ask any personal questions. I find her elegant.

She's just returned from a vacation at the Bay of Pigs. The Cuban beach was filled with the most beautiful yellow sand; she ate lots of coconut-fed pork. Now she's pointing her sun-tanned nose and slightly slanted eyes toward the sky. We're face to face, eye to eye. She suggests that we imagine a clear sky to help solve the mathematics problems. I agree and start thinking about a clear sky. We talk in class all the time but now we're silent. She points to the first evening stars, then, our heads turn to the grid squares. Who did she go to Cuba with? Her father, she says. Must be lying. She feels sexual. Jokingly, she mutters a few words in a language resembling Pali. My hand automatically moves to the paper and writes:

$$x = -2 +/- 2 \sqrt{2}$$

"Yes. Correct. See how we natives use just the clear evening sky to solve problems? I can feel my Mayan mathematics buzzing inside me. We got *zero* before them all." Rapidly, she's become a whiz in maths. Her numbers are innate, like the equations in the heads of sunflowers. My math skills are improving due to Deana. I am lucky. She explains every step in solving the problems, then she stands up. Spring is coming. Toronto will soon be one of the greenest cities in the world.

She's tall, stunning, confident, and doesn't have acrylic fingernail extensions. Deana points out, with a smile, that we're sitting in unceded territory that currently belongs to her people.

"Ages ago it was called simply Tkaronto after a legendary chief. Mohammed, have you noticed that we can't hear the sound of traffic in the park? Isn't that nice?"

"No traffic sounds at all."

Deana, at lunch or during break I forget which, recently told me that her ancestors used moonlight to help solve equations when trading beaver pelts with white fur-traders and their black-robed quangos from Quebec. At the time of contact, native shamans in the tribes were calculating the valency of the Hydrogen atom with just a feather held up to the wind. I keep in mind that she drives to class in a Tesla Model S. Her father is an important financier and developer of some kind.

On my notebook, in this mind-healing evening, I write down one binomial and polynomial after another. Deana and I are divinely connected through numbers but I don't think I should believe everything she says. When I look at her majestic face I feel moved, and somewhere deep inside I hear the sound track to the 1950s TV series, *The Last of the Mohicans* based on James Fenimore Cooper's 1826 novel. Why do I have this connection? I carry a negative stereotype of Indians like some Canadians, especially new Canadians. I freely admit this, but my view is changing due to knowing her—and this connection is certainly because, earlier, she told me that in Forest Hills she watched all 39 half-hour monochrome episodes of *The Last of the Mohicans* as part of her native schooling.

"All of us Indians watched it. We watched it to see how we were portrayed by the televisual whites. Necessary Native Semiotics. At least it wasn't boring like sex education. Only white guilt-ridden liberals think that it hurt us. The Mohicans were funny as hell."

We climb up a small hill and out of the park into the wind.

"Can I give you a drive home?"

"No, that's okay, I am not far. We'll meet tomorrow at class."

We've now moved past trigonometry. The trig vanished from our minds as soon as it stopped obeying Cosine Law and moved onto another area of math. We learn new areas of maths and almost at once forget what we learnt only a few weeks ago. You understand the integers, then the geometry, then the near abstractions, then the pure abstractions.

During a coffee break, I ask Deana: "What about this: find the 2 integers:

$x + y = 65$ x bear spirit and $x - y = 25$ x bear spirit$^{(2)}$?"

"Mo,' I think you have some bear spirit in you."

She shows me her calculations for how long a hammer takes to fall 3 meters on the moon. She supports the reasoning method with a question from her physics class, her calculation for the vertical velocity of a Great Blue Heron shot out of a canon at an angle of 35.0 degrees with an exit velocity of 25 m/s resulted in us sharing a moment.

We meet again at Cedarvale Park and this time we talk about the evolution of the words: "Indian," "native," "indigenous." She knows everything. The spring is nicely elongating. She's worn sandals. This is the first time since my arrival from Lahore that I've made a native friend. For some reason, they've avoided me all my Canadian life or perhaps it's because their visible presence in Toronto is almost zero, lost in the endless diversity. She seems to have affection for me. I think we're to be just friends. She's rich compared to me.

"What would happen if Ottawa gave the Assembly of First Nations a few trillion dollars: a one-time payment to fix all the imperialism, not to mention the dirty water in some communities? A few trillion? Let's say $2.5 x a10^(12) would that solve all the problems?" I ask.

"Problems solved."

"All colonial and moral questions have a solution. That solution is money. Money can solve all the bad that colonialism did. And, money can solve the guilt that whites imagine that they harbour. Maybe money can also cure spiritual land rights? Do you like Basmati rice?"

"Money can cure spiritual land rights, sure. When I was at university, a student from Lucknow—not Lucknow, Ontario—invited me to a dinner party at her house. I went before her guests came; she taught me how to cook Basmati rice with black cardamom, garlic, ginger, sticks of cinnamon all made in ghee. The smell was so beautiful that I fell on her couch and fainted. From then on I just didn't want to go back to eating smoky foods anymore. The fried Basmati rice *literally* made me leave some of my past behind. $2.5 x a10^(12) just might improve things. Great. Problem solved. Then we could take Iranian and Chinese cooking classes. As soon as I left my community I went to restaurants in Toronto, memorizing Korean menus, Japanese menus, Chinese menus. I even know most of the dishes made in Lahore. Ottawa should subsidize international cooking on the reserves. Eating macaroni and cheese, smoked bear, and cartilaginous moose filled with buckshot, and cooked with smoked Juniper berries and frozen McCain's fish is not good."

"What's your favourite Pakistani restaurant in Toronto." Most people say Little India on Gerrard East. Little India has the biggest collection of so-so south asian restaurants in Toronto. She asserts: "It is impossible to get a good south asian dinner on Gerrard East near Coxwell. For a good Pakistani meal one has to drive to Karachi Kitchen at 6560 Meadowvale Town Centre Circle, Mississauga."

"Do you think it would work to have an indigenous restaurant within Little India? I mean we're both sort of Indian, don't you think?"

"What would one call it?"

"I'll think about a name for an Indian restaurant in Little India." There will be more on my naming skills later.

From Forest Hills to Karachi, she has uttered an uncontested truth about south asian restaurants in Greater Tkoronto. A Pakistani dinner with proper naan can only be had in post-colonial Mississauga. She says: "The smell of kalongi in naan can heal our memory of small pox blankets."

"What's your favourite Japanese restaurant?"

"That would to be one in Yorkville, but it's too pretentious. I prefer Kibo Sushi House at 701 St. Clair West. To eat Japanese one doesn't have to drive to the sweltering tropical forests of Mississauga."

Deana is a prism. I feel like a half wavelength beside her. Why is she in adult high-school taking grade 12 math and science?

"Mo. Do you like painting?"

"Yes, I do. I know only some modern American stuff—the abstract paintings."

"Do you want to come with me to see an exhibition at the Art Gallery of Ontario?"

"Yes. When?"

"Friday?"

"Friday."

"Ok, I'll meet you at the front doors at noon."

"I can pick you up."

"Yes, that would be great."
She enters my address in her large iPhone.

3. Art Gallery of Ontario

Her Tesla has no buttons or dials whatsoever. All the indicators and controls are housed in a vertical monitor anchored to the dashboard. The car is as silent as a mosque on Sunday, and very fast. As soon as I relax in the sculpted seat, Deana asks: "I just got us tickets online. Mo', please don't tell me you have a membership to the gallery."

"I had a membership, but I haven't renewed it. I don't intend to renew it because it costs too much. I'll buy us lunch. What are we going to see?"

"Cecily Brown. She's on the fifth floor, the largest space."

The car drives us to the AGO while she gives me a pleasant in-Tesla lecture on Cecily Brown. Mellifluous sound waves pass from her beautiful mouth into my cochlea where it excites my Corti, which is filled with a potassium-rich fluid endolymph. I know, it isn't really a sexual organ but her effect on my hearing is stimulating.

Fantasy after fantasy builds in my ear. Her art history lesson is welcome because I know something about painting.

As usual, visiting with Deana causes some internet research. Cecily Brown is the daughter of David Sylvester, the British critic known for his commentaries on the twentieth-century Irish painter Francis Bacon who had painted several portraits of her father. It looks like Brown never forgot Bacon's bespectacled, screaming popes draped in purple robes hovering in black backgrounds. Bacon endlessly studied Diego Velázquez's 17th-century painting *Pope Innocent X*. Yet Bacon's 1953 ironic *Study after Velázquez's Portrait of Pope Innocent X* makes the pope into an open-mouthed screaming religious leader in a bird cage-like frame.

She says: "In my opinion Cecily Brown is a major figurative painter. Kind of abstract too. She puts figures that are not realistically painted in background scenes that are also not realistically painted either. It's very exciting work."

Images of gently running my fingers through Deana's black flowing hair flood my head via my endolymph. I need a break from her voice.

"I'd love to hear the sound quality in your car."

"CBC ok?"

"Sure, CBC is ok."

"Not another boring phone-in programme about gardening and fucking Calla Lilies." She touches the screen saying: "Minawaa giga-waabamin CBC." And then translates it for my benefit: "Goodbye CBC." The satellite radio station brings in stunningly clear versions of 50's and 60's Girl Groups. She turns down the volume.

Best sound system I've ever heard in a car. We're gliding down the rolling hills of Bathurst listening to The Shirelles singing *Will you love me tomorrow* and *Mama Said*, followed by The Marvelettes' *Please Mr. Postman* and *Beechwood 4-5789*.

Look: I am driving past the Holy Blossom Temple; people are wearing Tallits; the driver of the car is indigenous; she loves international cuisine; she has an iWatch; the Tesla is driving itself; it's 2024. There are no wars nearby, and I have clear drinking water at home. Deana wants to become a cosmopolitan New Canadian, and subtly, she's bopping to the music. Goodbye gasoline, hello lithium.

A mental note: Brown's slippery neo-realism produced depth, but not the depth that Anselm Kiefer's 6 x 8-metre canvases show. Kiefer's work reminds her of the European wars. In 1999, the Japan Art Association awarded Kiefer the *Praemium Imperiale*. This, along with the huge sales of his works, made him one of the richest artists in Germany. Brown, a woman, could never be expected to get such a prize or make anywhere near the same amount of money at that time.

I listen. I learn. I make mental notes:

—Brown likes abstract painters, Willem de Kooning in particular. de Kooning had a dick.

—All her influences are men.

—In the nineteen eighties some feminist art critics thought de Kooning was misogynist.

I can recall only one woman painter. I say: "I like Helen Frankenthaler."

"Is she the only woman painter you know?"

We park in front of the Ontario College of Art and Design University. This is a unique building. The institution is raised on stilts, a large box-shaped building with chess-boards painted on its sides, seeming to sit twelve metres above the ground, supported by pillars a few degrees off the vertical.

We take the elevator to the gymnasium-sized exhibition rooms. Deana instantly becomes lost in the paintings of Cecily Brown. At the far end of a vast exhibition space, she stands in front of a painting for eternity. What keeps her at this particular canvas? Does she intend for me to come and experience it with her? When I walk over, she brings her mouth near my ear. I feel the warmth of her breath. "Look at this one. A woman alone, near a window sill, on all fours, bum high up in the air, her head tracing a controlled arch reminiscent of edge-to-edge strokes of the Abstract Expressionists."

Why has she brought me to see this exhibition? She is playing with my endolymph. She intuits that I am alone, partnerless, childless, and that she can trick me into falling in love with her. For her amusement. Why were her lips so close to my ear? Intentional, must have been. It takes me a moment to recover from having her low breathy voice in my ear.

I stand in front of a painting of lovers holding each other and kissing in a dense forest filled with sunlight. On the horizon I can see an uplifting blue sky slatted by white trees and large flowers. Brown's painting recalls The Kiss, a morbid painting by Edvard Munch. Brown's and Munch's energy are similar: Both painters blur the faces of the lovers into agitated, featureless ovals. This visit is becoming a total twentieth century experience.

She drifts away to look at another Cecily Brown painting. I follow her, but slowly. Then she walks away again drawn to another painting. It's as if she is intentionally intoxicating herself on the paintings, yet her choreography feels deliberate. It is working on me. In small stages, I am drawn behind her like a Sardinian donkey. I try to get her to whisper in my ear again.

"Doesn't this one remind you of Gustave Courbet's *L'Origine du monde*? Deana points out the cream-coloured bums beside trees, women dressed like nuns, holding apart their vaginal lips in forests. The devil slides down to earth on one of Brown's rays of painted sunshine.

Another painting, *Boy Trouble*, depicts a young man holding his out-of-scale penis. A woman, legs apart, is getting ready to sit on it. Deana stands in front of this painting for ages. She wants to draw me next to her. I approach. She looks at me and smiles. I'm desperate to hear what she feels about this painting, but she's silent, and appears to be thinking critically. Tactical silence. I feel pulled closer to her. Should I rub my hand accidentally on purpose against her? I don't.

She has used the exhibition space to hook me. That's just a guess—because it's equally likely she is having a private experience from which I am excluded, only to admire and respect from afar. Can she make the content of these paintings become real? I doubt it. A tall security guard strolls by us.

We take the elevator down. Charged aurally and visually, and full of questions, I walk with her to the gallery shop. She purchases the Cecily Brown exhibition catalogue: $225.99. I look over her shoulder at this well-produced book which has many essays on Brown's work as well as tons of colour plates of other painters who had an impact on her. She was influenced by lots of men and only one woman: Joan Mitchell—but then this was an age, the last age of male-dominated painting. The men were: Willem de Kooning, Francis Bacon, Francisco de Goya, Rubens, Poussin, and one of the great European early abstract figurative painters, Oskar Kokoschka. Deana, glancing at the index, tells me James Ensor isn't mentioned in the catalogue.

I recognize a painting in the catalogue by a German Expressionist—Ernst Ludwig Kirchner. From my art school days, I remember a painting by him entitled: *Bathers at Moritizburg*, and for some strange reason I remembered the date: 1909. "Deana, do you think that Kirchner's painting was on Brown's mind? Looks like it was."

"That's what the paragraph I just glanced at says." Such an abrupt cut-off response. But there's nothing to it, I imagine.

In the lobby of the AGO we run into the curator, Penny Bill.

"Hello," Deana says. "Long time no see. How are you? What a great exhibition, thank you."

"You got the catalogue. Thank you. You'll get a laugh from my essay. Everything you already know."

"Penny, I'll love it. And, wow, Mary May Simon, Governor General of Canada blurbed it. I'll tell Dad I ran into you. He mentioned you recently."

"Give him my best wishes."

"I will. Bye."

"See you."

Deana wants us to have lunch at her favourite Chinese restaurant, Asian Legend on Dundas. The restaurant has two levels, one above and one below street level. We sit on the upper level. She orders without looking at the menu and asks for one bottle of Tsingtao. Artsy AGO patrons sit in the long row of tables with coats draped over a chair. It isn't long before the waiter comes to our table and sets down what we ordered.

"The garlic fried Tofu is great," she says lifting the beer bottle and pouring it into a tall glass. "What a clear beer, I love drinks that I can see through."

"Especially after those paintings. How do you know so much about Cecily Brown?"

"Did you like them?"

"I wouldn't have gone if you hadn't taken me. The sexual theme is a bit in your face."

"I suppose people find her paintings to be like that. But it isn't shocking in the context of modern art."

"Where did you study art?"

"Paris. Rome. And Oslo. Summer art history courses. You've crossed the pond? Obviously you have?"

"After high school I went to Europe with friends, that kind of thing, and I've been visiting friends in London for ages."

"Mo', I'm expecting a call from my Dad any minute now, won't take long." A waiter places garlic tofu, shrimp dumplings, sticky rice and a $54 California Bass on our table.

"Mo', here's Dad. Two seconds, sorry." Before she picks up her phone, I accidentally glance the screen. The name Azaadi displays. Azaadi is an Urdu word, I can't remember what it means.

"Dad, hi. Nice to hear you. Just having lunch with a friend. Can I call you back in a bit?"

His voice, just loud enough for me to hear, is loving and rounded: "Okay dear—talk in a bit."

"Mohammed, regarding Europe: I have to tell you, I'm visiting my dad in Marseille."

"Oh … when are you going?"

"Flight's this Friday. I'll be back in about a month or so."

"I won't see you for a such a long time."

"Not that long, I'll be back soon. Maybe sooner than a month."

She's detected my sinking heart at once. Her game of making me walk to where she was standing in the gallery has worked. I'm sure she's playing with me. She knows I'm older—too old to have a relationship with her. She knows she's beautiful; she must feel sure that nothing will happen. We'll be the kind of friends who share her interests: arts, astronomy and Chinese food.

She chugs the last drops of transparent beer, and we walk down the restaurant steps onto a busy Dundas. A TTC street car floats by. There's the Tesla, still looking perfect. She reaches into her over-the-shoulder Louis Vuitton Speedy and touches a button. The gull doors lift slowly. She carefully places the catalogue on the back seat. The three-phase induction motor plasters me into the seat and we zip up Bathurst, past the synagogues and churches right to Chaplin Avenue.

She knows I'm looking at her. She has some kind of indigenous power over my fluids.

We've arrived at my apartment building. I don't have the courage to invite her in. My place is small, whistle-clean like the interior of her Tesla. A silent impasse. I look across at her sitting behind the wheel. I look at her hands, her face, her indigenous body enclosed by a private-school white shirt, her legs enveloped in fishnet stockings. My emotional heaviness becomes apparent. She slides her hand over mine, leans over and gives me an innocent hug. The car door rises magically and she says she'll see me in a bit. Silently, the Tesla carries her away.

Our term ended, she has left to spend some time in Marseille. With her father, she said. At one of our meetings she mentioned her attachment to astronomy. I ran out and purchased the exact brand of binoculars she said she had: *Canon 10 x 42mm IS L Water Proof.*

And now, it's that Friday of her departure at 15:45. I can't be accused of stalking her because she gave me her flight number and told me about an online air traffic tracking programme. On my screen, a tiny model airplane in red is her Air France flight. I wait a bit, then go outside and point the binoculars up. I scan the skies above Toronto, hoping to see her A380 climb into the Western Hemispheric air. It's heading northeast toward Ottawa: There she is in a metal burka with large engines on either side. She enters my view, I watch the online symbol move in a succession of imperceptible jerks across the screen. Goodbye Deana …

I can't help feeling that she used the AGO gallery space to colonize me, to transform me into a satellite circling her. I suspect that actually touching Deana is bound to be memorable, and as the days roll on I spent my time listening to *I Gotta Dance To Keep From Crying* by Smokey Robinson. Bien sûr, there were occasional emails giving, jour à jour, les details plat; regardless, each email from Deana made me miss her like mad. I remembered she had a nice smell. She did not smell like smoked moose or elk, but Baccarat Rouge 540 Extrait de Parfum. I noticed the bottle in her open purse. I looked up the price. The scent lingered in my nose like the way the cave paintings have lingered in Lascaux.

4. Deana's place

She's back from France. A new term of maths with Deana starts. Again, I get a chance to sit near but not next to Deana. After class, we have lunch, about twice a week, at either the nearby Somali or Korean restaurant.

"So what was the food like in the south of France?" Deana, without looking at her mobile, lists in perfect mid-Atlantic French: "Olives picholines or luques; oursins; chestnut honey; forgot the word in French sorry; fricandeau, dorade; étoiles, a kind of sea snail; figatelli, a sort of liver salami, usually Corsican; Picpoul wines—Creyssels, Beauvignac. And, I'm not done yet, duck fat fries; raw mussels; Cabécou burgers—tons of these."

"And Pélardon and Rocamadour, soft raw milk goat cheeses also. I thought about you."

By the end of term, Chandri, the Assamese woman, and I have also become good class mates. With Chandri I speak Urdu daily. My linguistic skills impress Deana, and she has learned to count in Urdu.

Chandri gets over 95% on all her tests. She shows me the steps to solving problems but I am still only hitting 75%.

At the end of March break, Paul sets the final exam for 16 April at 0930. My cystoscopy is on the same day at 07:30 in the morning. At the end of the class, I approach his desk looking worried.

"I have a doctor's appointment on the same day as the exam. Can I sit the exam another time either before or after, please?"

"Can you change the appointment?"

"I'm sure my surgeon will not be able to accommodate."

The word *surgeon* has an arresting effect on him. This is Canada—the country of universal healthcare.

"I can show you an email exchange I had with his secretary about attempting to change the date? This a confidential matter."

Paul has accepted my reason. "Sure, an email would do it. I just need to see it in case the administration asks for proof." The next day, I show him the printed email with the word *cytology* blackened out by me. He glances at the two pages. "Ok, no problem at all."

Outside, a few blocks from school in front of an Ethiopian grocery store, I tell Deana that I am coming down with a really bad cold and will not be in class for the exam.

"Doctor listened to my lungs and said it might be pneumonia. Confirmation pending."

"Hope not. That could be serious. Have they got you on antibiotics?"

"I have to take them for ten days. And, Paul's accepted a note from my doctor."

She puts her hand on my shoulder and leaves it there. "Mo', there's nothing to worry about. These doctors are the real artists, they're better than visual artists. I'm going to visit my dad and mum anyway. We'll vape the medicine pipe so you'll recover as soon as possible."

I've become comfortable looking non-stop into her eyes. "Deana, at the beginning of class I hated the daily land acknowledgements, but after getting to know you I look forward to hearing them every day. I almost feel like standing up but I just can't. What exactly will you vape?"

"We're going to smoke *Indigenous Grass*. It's a new brand. My dad is cultivating it with some native botanists. Mohammed, we'll smoke some for your health."

"Thank you, I'm sure it'll help. Deana, a question has been on my mind. Just wondering: Do Jewish settlers in Palestine acknowledge that the land on which they gather is the traditional territory of the Palestinians? The land in question was the Kingdom of Judah and the Kingdom of Israel wasn't it?"

"I wouldn't tell Palestinians emigrating to Canada that they were about to become settlers." She's always one step ahead of me.

The class ends. I get 76%. Without Deana's help and not to mention Chandri's, my grade would have been 65%—better than my high school grades decades ago.

I continue seeing Deana for a lunch or dinner here and there, but our meetings have become infrequent. Perhaps our connection is ending. I don't feel close enough to ask her why this bit-by-bit distance has set in. Then, three months later her name appears on my screen. I push the glass with the tip of my finger:

"Mohammed, I know you're going to tell me you're fine, aren't you?"

"I'm fine, Deana."

"You forgotten all the maths?"

"No. I haven't forgotten anything."

"How did you do in physics?"

"I did well. Got 86%."

The short chat leads me to a temporary waiting room outside heaven. Feels good to hear her voice again. I haven't stopped thinking about her. She knows it. Her sentences are filled with confidence. I ask: "Lunch next week? Asian Legend? I know you're going to order clear beer and deep-fried garlic Tofu."

"Yeah, sure. Mo', I got great news. I got a transparent fiberglass canoe."

"You'll be able to see the bottom of the lake."

"And, Mohammed, I got a super large telescope—381mm. I didn't tell you about my hobby since I was a kid. I go to star-gazing parties."

"Is that large? I don't know."

"Large enough to see all the beautiful arms of galaxies. But I have to be under a dark sky. I can show some even under a polluted sky like Toronto. Let's stay in touch."

"Okay. Yes, stay in touch."

I put down the phone, then on my 27 inch iMac I start looking up astronomy sites. I must give her the impression that I know a little bit. Otherwise she'll go silent again, though I wonder why she really went silent.

My research takes me to many sites showing me how the heavens work and how telescopes extend the collective sight of humanity into the deep past. Little bits from the physics come back to me. Yellow stars are cooler than white stars which are super-hot. I didn't know what a light year is or was or if we're in one now. Also, the universe has a gravitational constant that is true everywhere. It's:

$$6.67430 \times 10^{\wedge}(-11) \ Nm^{\wedge}(2) \ / \ kg^{\wedge}(2)$$

Feels like Light Years until I see her again. A mini-fraction of one of those years goes by and she's still on my mind. My phone vibrates, it's her name on the strengthened Gorilla Glass of my iPhone SE. Perhaps there's conflict in her agenda. She's calling to cancel. Fuck. She's calling to cancel. I sense a trickster. But the fact—and it's a fact—that she's called me twice in one day. Even if it's a cancellation it really isn't a cancellation, it will be an rescheduling of auditory fluids. I'll get excited just listening to her voice.

"Hi, Deana."

"Mohammed. Hi. Are you busy later tonight?"

"I'm doing nothing."

"Can you come over? I can show you some of the night sky. You can fly up to the sky."

"Deana, you didn't tell me you were a member of the Royal Astronomical Society of Canada?"

"What? How do you know that?"

"I saw your archived posts—you raised some interesting points."

"Researching—were you? I'll text you my address."

Moments later, my phone vibrates for a third time: Maybe she's got cold feet about inviting me over. I look at the glass: It's a Conference Call from Zero and One. I've been saved by real-estate.

"Mohammed, good time to have a chat?" Zero asks.

Before I can respond, One interrupts. "Mohammed, good time to have a chat?"

"Nice to hear from you both. What's up?"

One says: "Remember that fourteen-unit building way outside Toronto?"

"Yes."

Zero announces: "We got it. After the inspector's report we got the price reduced somewhat."

"Lots of repairs to do?" I ask.

"We got ten percent knocked off the asking price," Zero says. "Now, Mohammed, here's an easy question, and stay calm: What did we pay for the building if their ask was $2.2 mil? Don't use your calculator. And, just letting you know that we're going to keep their current management company. This way you'll not be dealing with loads of tenants."

"I see."

"You sound glum," One says.

"What's my role in all this?" I ask.

"Your role is to keep an eye on the management company," One says. "Check their numbers—spot check month to month, when you feel like. We're confident with your mathematical abilities."

"You've given me a promotion?"

"Promoted, and less work. Do you want to go to the same restaurant?" One asks.

"One million, nine-hundred and eighty dollars," I say.

"You used your calculator," they say in unison.

It is now ten o'clock in the morning. According to my calculation, I have to wait ten hours until I see her. Early this evening, I catch the number 7 Bathurst bus down to Helena Avenue. I walk 450 metres to Wychwood and down to Zanzibar Street. I walk along this street until I hit Helena again, and then back to Wychwood. I sit in the park in front of her apartment building and on my phone watch Erin Burnett's *Out Front* on CNN. For some strange reason she is interviewing my favorite CNN host Don Lemon. (Breaking Future News: Don Lemon will soon get fired from CNN.) At 19:55 I shut off Don and start my voyage to her apartment lobby. I am nervous as shit. The principal question: has she tricked me into keeping her company and will she get involved with me in other ways? With that thought in mind, I push the buzzer numbers she texted. A muffled yet recognizable voice says: "Hello Mo'. C'mon up." The glass door clicks open, I walk to the elevator and press the floor she texted. I raise my hand to knock on her door and then stop. What if she asks me about why I left Montreal? Perhaps I'd say: I lived there for for 36 years. I left. The province is the most ethnically nationalistic in Canada. I had moved to Toronto in 2015 but the following date sticks in my head: 29 January 2017. In my apartment, while watching CBC on my computer and eating chicken curry, mint chutney, brown basmati rice and buttered basin key roti, the news came as a shock: Alexandre Bissonnette, unquestionably indigenous to la belle province, shot and killed six muslims in Québec City. Thankfully, I was in Toronto and not within the range of Quebec's clinically depressed ethnic nationalists. I'd said *bon débarras*, and took the train back to Ontario.

Peacefully, my knuckles make contact with her door.

I must avoid dissing her culture.

"What happened? Did the elevator get stuck?"

I see a nice spread on the table and a bottle of Languedoc Blanc "Pierres d'Argent." I make a mental note to find out the price later on the LCBO website. Bad habit.

"Here's my new telescope. I haven't put in the eyepiece yet."

"I know what an eyepiece is. And I even know that we should be able to see the part of Perseus that leads to the Double Cluster a massive collection of low magnitude stars."

"I'm surprised you've done this research."

"I am trying to impress you. Anyway, I have an interest in all this. Remember, I passed physics."

The night slowly falls. The light pollution somehow goes away but doesn't.

"Mo' here, I'll point this north-west to Mirfak then we move out through Perseus toward Cassiopeia and here is the Double Cluster: Take a look."

"Okay, let me have a look. I'll move to the eyepiece." I stare into the dark sky, I see just a few pinpoints of starlight, nothing exciting.

"I don't see much. Lovely stars."

"Keep looking." I continue staring into the reflector's focuser, then slowly something happens as she moves the scope through an empty dark field: I begin to see two sets of stars of subtle colour collected up there in the nearly black sky. I find I can't look away—must be all those years I spent behind a camera. I can't look away from the beautiful composition she's made. Slowly, her composition is drifting out of view.

We leave the telescopes on the balcony in Toronto's pretend night sky. I follow her into her dark room. She turns on a small light. A tidy bedroom with a cream coloured asian-style mattress on the floor, a chest of drawers, some folded clothes on table. We lay down. Despite not knowing each other well, we hold each other tightly and then unravel. The night passes quickly, then her phone wakes us. She kisses the back of my neck, checks her texts, emails, news and says: "Let's go look at the sun, it should be above the atmospheric haze by now."

"An eclipse?"

"No, that's on Monday, 8 April, 2024, nearly a total solar eclipse in Toronto. We'll be able to see 99.56 percent of it from here. Coffee?"

"Please."

"How did you sleep?"

"I slept deeply, but your mattress felt like granite." She smiles and leaves the room to make coffee. I linger on her bed for a few moments. This friendship will be about looking up. I can't see any down side. Not yet.

"Are you coming?" I notice the pattern on the mattress. They are coloured drawings of planets in a night sky filled with small stars. I've fallen in love.

She's on her balcony, with a smaller telescope. The coffee is clearing my head.

What's she up to now?

"It's daylight. I don't see any stars."

"Mo', you look nice in the morning. It's a solar telescope with a hydrogen alpha filter."

"Hydrogen what? We'll go blind in two seconds."

"Mo', You won't go blind. It's juicy blood-orange red, you'll like it. I've put in a zoom eyepiece, take a look."

My face brushes against her face as we trade places for a turn at the eyepiece which shows me a massive, bright red spherical globe filled with red rivers, tiny black sun spots splattered here and are grouped in little island clusters. "The sun looks heavy," I say.

"Heavy, I agree but it's suspended in all that blackness?"

"Gravity must be black, I guess."

The Prominences look like still snakes which don't seem to move; some resemble red stick figures walking along the limb of the sun. These stringy lines coming out of the sun don't move, or are they moving slowly? I'm loving the view but need a break. I lift my head from the eyepiece and look at a green park nearby, trees bathed sunlight. Is it really the same sunlight I'm seeing? Deana is wearing a yellow coloured shirt. "Deana, I see a solar prominence in the shape of a man walking and holding up what looks like the Albania flag with the colours flipped. How high is it going to rise?"

"Albania? I don't know about Albania, but the prominence is already about 200,000 kilometres long."

I look through the eyepiece and hear robins and cardinals singing in the sunny hydrogen. I feel Deana's lovely cool hand on my back. "Deana, it looks like the stringy thing is breaking away from the sun. I'm not kidding: the thing is really detaching from the sun."

"You might get lucky and actually see it vanish into space."

"Lucky?" I ask. She doesn't answer my question. She's allowing me time to concentrate on what I'm seeing. The prominence flutters, becomes a Coronal Mass Ejection, and vanishes into the surrounding pitch black field called gravity. I did get lucky.

"Soon, it might arrive on Earth. Mo', you'll see all those stick figures as green Auroras, probably destroying our communications systems."

That evening, during my late night walk, solar winds convert into bright wavy green curtains over Toronto. My cellphone still works. I recommend Rogers Communications to all my friends.

5. Thought experiments to reduce the pain

I'VE BEEN HERE at least thirty times. The routine is acceptable because it's life-saving. I take the northbound bus to a hospital which has a department called Urology Park. Ridiculously, this unit boasts an internal waterfall that trickles down a high stairway leading to the area where bladders are treated. The swishing of a thin sheet of water over granite-like stone relaxes everyone's bladders in Bladder Central.

I walk into the waiting room. It's filled with patients, some older, some younger, but with one thing in common. A bladder, a sick bladder. I approach the receptionist. Her desk sits high over a waterfall that flows endlessly to Lake *Entohouron*, then through the traditional territories of the Haudenosaunee, the Anishinabek, the Montagnais, the Cree, the Mi'kmaq to the sea. The receptionist doesn't need to ask for my health card anymore. I simply extend my wrist and she places a white plastic hospital band around it and asks me to wait. I watch the 24-hour news with everyone else who's waiting. An elderly man in a wheelchair is rolled in by a hospital volunteer. He has a black patch over his eye. Maybe he has eye as well as bladder cancer. A senior citizen volunteer wears red high heels that click with authority on the hard plastic floor. The sound helps me stay distracted and not preoccupied with the coming pain. Julian the apostate, whom you'll meet in a few minutes, is the patron saint of bladder cancer. He'll cure us of the affliction.

Self-pity fills me. A *National Geographic* has a special section on a White Rhino being operated on for bladder cancer, and on the next page, for some strange reason, there are historical photos of Obama at the Wazir Khan Mosque in downtown

Toronto. It's a world-wide fact that doctors' waiting rooms are the graveyards for old, infection-carrying magazines. I open the germ-loaded *National Geographic* to pages where zoo vets are giving the rhino two litres of tranquilizer before they insert a laser-tipped catheter which is just a little larger in diameter than the one I am about to experience.

I experience two kinds of catheters: either a 17-French flexible cystoscope with a 5.7 mm diameter, or a 22-French rigid cystoscope with a 70-degree lens and a 7.3 mm diameter. Both hurt like hell. The catheters with a camera and/or laser on the end of it up my dick like a snake; then a few minutes later the snake is withdrawn and I am back on the bus heading home to drink lots of water and tea. On the bus, I hear a Quebecois accent intersect with one from Dakar; *sans-faute*, the sub-equatorial African French is easier to comprehend.

For me to go on living, the examination I'm about to describe must take place every three months. It will happen for the rest of my life or until recurrent, papillary tumors on the dome of my bladder go away—Dr. Helena Bar says they're superficial. And now, three months after my last appointment, Dr. H. Bar is about to do some routine camera work after the nurse helps me lie on the metal table. The insertion begins. "I'm going in now," she says. When I wince, Dr. H. Bar slowly withdraws the scope and releases saline into my urethra. It is time for me to construct a day-dream. She breaks my dream as soon as it's established. "Okay, here we go." This is said gently, with a note of reassurance.

On the colour monitor above my head I see a pink cavern with a dark, centrally located, oval geometry. It's my imperative to stay distracted, otherwise it all becomes too painful to bear, especially if she has to do laser ablations. I hear a nice distracting song in my memory: *All I Have To Do Is Dream* by the Everly Brothers. Sometimes, during laser zaps, nurse Musafareen holds my hand.

The key is to dream up places, people, and events of centuries ago, far away from the reality of Musafareen's warm hand. This is hard to do because without the tethering effect of her hand I would float away on a day-dream leaving Dr. H. Bar holding my dick.

Her hands have inserted a limp flexible cable with a lens on the end up my dick in a hospital in Canada. We come here to be saved not to die, as is the case in places such as South Asia and Africa and South America where public hospitals are waiting rooms to convert fixable living bodies into bodies placed on blocks of broken ice, with vultures filling the trees outside waiting for a snack. Here, in Canada, the majestic hospital buildings have the names of donors proudly affixed to exterior walls. This is not a useful fantasy to escape into but for the anchoring tug of Musafareen's hand. Every year or so, a resection will be required, but only if Dr. H. Bar identifies a tumour that can't be *dusted* with her laser. The uncertainty is haunting. I am in pathogen-city.

A day-dream: My bladder is a fleshy, pink piggy bank, occupying my body like a newly emerged autonomous republic filling up with Solidus, a Roman coin of nearly solid gold, from the time of the emperor Julian the Apostate, who was born in 331, and died 363, aged 31. These facts have a destabilizing effect; they keep me in a world of certainties. Documents from the Late Roman Empire show that Julian survived bladder cancer but was wounded in the Battle of Samarra, near Maranga. He lies in Istanbul. According to the mathematics of that era, the Roman Cosmological Constant is:

$$3.63 \times 10^{-11} \text{ Nm}^2 / \text{kg}^2$$

and here's the relationship between battles and splotchy bladder carcinoma:

E = M _ bladder C^(2) RC

Thought experiments are a work of art. Julian, the patron saint of bladder cancer, was the last non-Christian ruler of the Roman Empire, canonized on the basis of his Christian years. But, alas, I digress: I like going for cystoscopies in the Roman Empire. Julian married Helena, the daughter of the previous emperor, Constantius, whose name means "constancy." These are reassuring. I'm being operated on in an open-air Roman amphitheatre; white stone columns, tall as Douglas Firs, rise into the Mediterranean sky. I can smell fresh fish. A Canadian surgeon, of Italian descent, flown in from Woodbridge, Ontario, will operate. The assistants call him Claudio. The threat of the laser brings vultures from grasslands of Africa into my head; they hover over the Italian sky. Black wings in the sky twitch to correct paths that might lead them to a meal of my rotten bladder and all.

I'm the subject of a demonstration bladder operation at the prestigious Scuola Medica Privata de Roma. Rows of students, much better dressed than the students in Saint Mungo's, wearing the latest clothes from Milan, look on. Now, a Greek doctor assisting the Canadian has, in his hand, a long snake-like tube with a tiny red light on its end. I have forgotten his name. No, I haven't. His name is Snakeopolis Pitosis. As he approaches my penis, the instrument's electric cord disconnects from HydroRoma: it's lights out in the Greco-Roman world of Julian, the Neoplatonic emperor.

The fall or maybe the spring equinox is the best time for cystoscopies; it's when things work in favour of Julian the Apostate and all his patients because we isolate the Roman Constant:

RC = E / M _ bladder C ^(2)

The thought experiments make things pleasant. In the past, I've had Bacillus Calmette-Guerin (BCG) immunotherapy to treat some non-invasive bladder tumours, nine installations of 50 mg. Nine calendar catheters. This means that, once the nurse has put in 50 mg of the BCG, I'll have to hold my pee for two hours after the catheter has been put in. I don't pee. I don't pee on the bus going home. I don't pee at home. The pressure builds up. This BCG treatment has happened eight times. I come home. I don't pee. At precisely 12:01 I pee with such force that I enter low orbit.

Dr. H. Bar sees nothing impressive, but a small recurrent papillary tumour. This information doesn't make me feel broken or sad. The news could be worse. I've learnt to leave feeling well after every cytology that reveals only minor cancerous encroachments. I'll have to come back soon for a full-on resection.

6. Salam France

"HI DAD. ÇA VA?"

"I'm fine. What are you up to?"

"I'm walking along Bloor Street. Beautiful blue sky. Wish you were here. Michel Houellebecq and Bernard-Henri Lévy are speaking at the Anne Tanenbaum Centre."

"Cool. These guys are *true* public intellectuals. Except in America. I tried to model you on them."

"Dad, I am not a man. I'll be going into an elevator so we may go offline for a bit."

"Maybe something nice will happen."

"Okay, I'm sitting at the back of the lecture hall waiting for this gig to start. Totally renovated lecture space."

"Saudi donation, bet you," her father says. "Deana. Lost you for a second. What's the conference about?"

"Not a conference. Onstage interview. The host is Dr. Bernard-Henri Lévy. Dad, holy shit, he's that super famous guy from France. Who's on CNN all the time. Fareed Zakaria interviews him non-stop. He's now a visiting professor at U of T. Sssh, it's starting …"

A silence in the lecture hall as Michel Houellebecq and Dr. Bernard-Henri Lévy saunter onto the stage. Houellebecq, wearing a light blue shirt with a worn leather jacket, rotates the chair 360 degrees before sitting down in it. Little flourish of style. Dr. Lévy is wearing a white shirt which is slightly unbuttoned.

"Dad, can you follow online? Says here it will be on YouTube in real time."

"Sure, I'll watch it with you. Send the link."

In front of an audience of about fifty Global Politics students, Michel Houellebecq and Bernard-Henri Lévy take their places on the low-rise stage. They sit in leather swivel chairs on either side of a low round table under spotlights.

Dr. Lévy, in an assertive, beautifully elongated English, reads the Land Acknowledgment:

"Out of respect for the Indigenous peoples of Canada, we acknowledge that we are on traditional territories of the Wendat, the Anishinabek (a-ni-shna-bek) Nation, the Haudenosaunee (hoh-Dee-noh-Shoh-nee) Confederacy, and the Mississaugas of the Credit First Nations. We also recognize the enduring presence of all First Nations, Métis, and Inuit people in Ontario and the rest of Canada."

Dr. Lévy put the typed sheet face-down on the table with a Gallic shrug. He looks like he had years of experience connecting with audiences. Now, he outlines from memory Michel Houellebecq's literary projects over the last two decades, ending with his recent book which, Lévy says mischievously, presents Islam as backward. This is fact, Deana thinks. The popular French author, Houellebecq, invents stories in which French citizens, having become French politicians, use procedures in the assembly to make laws that Islamify certain regions of France where Muslims are in the majority. Some majority Muslim areas are actually attempting to pass laws that forbid the local development of pig farms. Deana remembers that the book she read with her father had a comic touch set in complex, beautifully-written fiction. His works are even studied in university courses outside the French-speaking world. Under Islam, in Houellebecq's loopy vision, France reverts to the pre-Revolutionary era. And, in this context, Dr. Lévy, continuing to mischievously spark a debate, mentions the tragic murder of Daniel Pearl, a *Wall Street Journal* reporter who was tortured and murdered by intellectuals in a Muslim militia group in Karachi. The reference to Daniel Pearl puts the discussion in a larger geopolitical frame.

"Dad. Lévy has his shirt undone nearly down to his belt. Can you see that? Merde."

"Hairless. That takes courage. The courage of style, however, it's just stylistic. Imagine if I dressed like that."

"Dad, don't."

"It's the viewpoint that takes courage. Does he have what it takes to stick his neck out?"

The lecture hall contains smartly dressed students and professors, a few kippas and hijabs. The discussion flows in English punctuated by French asides. Houellebecq's English is good but grammatically tipsy. Regarding Islam, Houellebecq takes up Lévy's dare and expresses his own personal shock regarding the terrorist attack of 7 January 2015 when Islamic terrorists killed several people at *Charlie Hebdo*, the French satirical magazine.

"I am horrified when I think of this event of only a few years ago, caused simply by the publication of some harmless cartoons of Mohammad," Lévy responds expertly connecting with his audience. But now a question: "When you are constructing your fictional characters, do you not enter a research phase in which you identify almost completely with them? And if so, and I suspect it is so, the question that emerges is the following: Were you temporarily, one could safely say, *un peu Islamique*, during that phase of writing?"

"We're all a bit like the characters we invent, *non*? I mean, in some way or another. Writing a book is like looking in the mirror, and bien sûr this is, a distorting *miroir* which contorts perspective along with a point of view. *N'est pas?* So, Bernard, you want these people to consider I am like the people I invent in my book? Well, yes. I mean I have to be; otherwise I could not actually make characters with flesh and bones. They'd be just puppets that I use to push particular views. And that is incoherent. Yet, it might seem strange to readers of my works to think that I am against inventing characters for straight forward political reasons. So, concluding, yes, I become a Muslim. *Temporairement, islamique, oui bien sûr.* I design a literary work in order to—what's the word in English—I don't know. To step inside another culture's experience—*quelque chose comme ça.*" Dealing with the vagaries of public opinion is his expertise.

Bernard Lévy nods thoughtfully and taps the theme along. "Certain kinds of characters are developed by a certain kind of imagination, and this process reveals a view of the world possessed by the particular writer. So, naturally, I don't think it's wrong to impute ideological settings to the author. I, myself, write about an outmoded, primitive religion that has become an integral part, a very concrete part of state-craft in many places on the earth. That is not a pretty sight to say the least. But I have to do it."

"Generally, authors are detached—so they claim—from the characters and ideologies they invent; yet strangely, the characters extend the imagination of the author, at the risk of negatively extending the vision of book. *Je veux dire* it is an advantage to concoct *l'autre,*" Houellebecq says artfully.

The conversation flows without the typical theoretical antagonism that Deana sees on French television. Bernard Pivot comes to mind. Lévy, in this context, is in masterful control of the flow of ideas, gently re-over-focusses the discussion.

"How, then, do you manage to write your way out the mind-frames of certain characters, especially of the Islamic protagonists?"

"Well, you take good strong coffee and wake up from being a Muslim. You launch yourself back into modern, post-nineteen-sixties Catholic France. What a wonderful feeling to actually be in someone else's shoes, especially if the shoes are from from Pakistan."

Their dialogue deepens an understanding of the process of writing sociologically and politically. This talk, Deana thinks, is a welcome uplift from the hyper-policed debates taking place. Dad must be enjoying the intellectual stimulation, up in Muskoka. Dr. Lévy crosses hectares of history and politics and religion, landing us right into the question/answer period. At this talk, like many public talks at U of T, it is the procedure for questions from the audience to be written on pieces of paper submitted to the chair of the discussion. That way, nobody will say something that offends a group. The question must show who wrote it and be an agreement to having the name disclosed publicly. A student, microphone in her pocket, walks up and down the rows to collect the questions. The questions are taken to Dr. Lévy who stylishly puts on his reading glasses—the man makes an event out of every single gesture—and reads through the questions, dividing them into two piles on the round table. At no time does he disconnect from his audience. He continually lowers his glasses to look at us, change his facial gestures making this a delightful passage of time. "Please don't worry. No censorship. This is just done to condense the questions," he says moving his hands to illustrate the word condense. The audience is charmed, despite these control mechanics.

"Tricia has asked: *Mr Houellebecq: When you make characters that look and feel like your persona, do you feel like Diego Velázquez's Las Meninas?*"

"*Alors*, Michel Houellebecq, *tu es intrigué?*" Dr. Lévy asks.

"The question must be from an art historian. Yes, I appreciate that painting very much. I don't believe that back then he would have thought of himself as a huge artist or anything like that—I mean the same way we see ourselves as great artists and writers in today's world. Velázquez would have been considered a gifted craftsman who was brought into the court to do a job, nothing more—*rien de plus. Mais, au contraire*, I'm a pre-framed, framed and post-framed author who is a media personality. This framing happening automatically by social media et cetera. I can't but help looking into a mirror every second of my life." Fawning laughter flutters through the audience. "*Non, non attends*, I haven't finished: If you are reading and perhaps even studying my works perhaps you could refer to Rousseau 1772 and 1776. He set up a dialogue with himself. I've gotten some inspiration from *Rousseau juge de Jean-Jacques*. The urge for writers to invent protagonists with large world views is huge, that urge never goes away. Rousseau's multiple personality, self-consciousness, monologic self-understanding, *et tout ça*. That is how I work."

The smartly dressed student, clearly an anglophone, possibly aware of Houellebecq's reputation, is given the microphone: "I am writing my thesis on your works. May I have an interview? My name is Tricia. I'm in the French department. Thank you."

"Yes, I'll be here long enough to be interviewed. Your doctorate will increase sales of my works. Thank you." More laughter from the students and profs.

Dr. Lévy holds up a second question slip and adjusts his glasses. "And now we have a question from a Toronto writer, Mohammed E. Smith. What a pleasure, Mr. Smith. I've read *The Reformation*. I admire the proposition of your book: that a modified Islam can make a contribution to the West. This consideration is valuable because it gently brushes against Michel Houellebecq's point of view."

Dr. Lévy gazes into the audience, with controlled elegance, sweeps off his glasses. "*Voilá*, here are two questions: First: *Do you think that any areas in France will be governed by Islamic laws in combination with French laws or will French laws predominate?* And the second question: *Were there any historical factors involved in the Charlie Hebdo massacre? Très pénétrant.* Thank you for seeking clarity."

Houellebecq, looking bored, responds as if he's heard this exact same question countless of times before: "Mr. Smith, may

I say that I too have read your book. I find it naive beyond belief. 'Belief' being the operative word. And I find it irrelevant in any case. I can't remember all the arguments. Sorry I can't be more helpful."

Dr. Lévy nods approval to the patrolling student who offers a large red microphone to Mohammed E. Smith.

"Thank you for the insightful exchange and I appreciate your criticism of *The Reformation*. About the *Charlie Hebdo* massacre, might this event be connected with France's past? Just wondering. You know Congo, Algeria and all that."

"It is not connected with France's past. This is to do with democracy. We have a functional version of it in France and here in Toronto. Islam does not like democracy. Yes, sure, you all say Algeria this, Algeria that. For how long are certain French citizens going to go on using Algeriaism as an excuse for not fully condemning the vicious killings of utterly innocent satirical writers? Blame France for the Islamic dictators? That's—how you say? a jerk knee reflex. You want to make an issue of French colonialism. Okay. Why not Africanism, Ugandaism, and why not, Icelandism?" Things are becoming like on French television.

Dr. Lévy looks at Houellebecq and says:"*Vous trouve tout ça comique? Moi aussi.*" The audience is silent, perhaps fearing that a bomb will go off.

Deana notices that Dr. Lévy, has undone another shirt button. The discussion has him heated, but he remains expertly calm. Mohammed. It can't be. What's he doing here? How did he get to be an author? He can't even solve simple quadratic equations, and he's popped up again.

"First, let's be clear: I don't support what happened at *Charlie Hebdo*. How do you explain the persistent, long-term anger within France? *Charlie* pokes fun at Muslims more than any other group."

Houellebecq interrupts: "Your statement is false. *Hebdo* makes fun of all religious groups. What you're saying is false. *Ce n'est pas vrai.*"

"Moreover, *Hebdo* has made and does make fun of the Jewish religion. They have made offensive fun at Jews," Lévy says.

"The intensity of their comic attacks on Islam is necessary, I agree with you. But there should be a balanced sense of comedy. I think *Hebdo* was not as comically intense on Jews."

"False. *Ce n'est pas vrai,*" Houellebecq says calmly.

"So, Mr. Smith, what would satisfy you as a balanced sense of humour?"

"Thank you for your question, Dr. Lévy. Perhaps they could publish cartoons of the current Israeli head of state in a novel sexual position in Yad Vashem. That might balance things."

Someone whispers the word *arrogant*.

"Mr. Mohammed. Thank you very much. We've spent enough time on this." After a few other less intense questions, the on-stage interview concludes. Deana rushes out. Stunned, she heads out onto Bloor Street. To distract herself, she sets out to buy a new 0.9mm pencil with 2B leads. She can never find both items together in in any single art supply store and she usually ends up ordering them from Amazon.ca.

She heads toward a stationery store near Bathurst. Mohammed's reserved, balanced, impudent voice in the lecture hall won't leave her. A few days ago, she was kissing him. Today, she discovers that she might be starting to date an unknown Toronto novelist. With a dual personality in adroit balance it's impossible to tell who the fuck he is. Before she felt like she'd hit a mini cultural jack pot in knowing Mohammed: Her father was going to like him because her Dad loves outsiders more than insiders. Also Mohammed is a little weird, another plus. But why wasn't he honest?

She comes to a needed rest on a bench in Philosophers Walk. She reaches into her bag and calls her father: "Dad, my math friend, Mohammed. That was him pinning Houellebecq against the wall. He's not the Mo' in math class. I feel betrayed. I got taken in by his false humility. I've been duped into helping him with his math, not to mention … But at least he doesn't undo his shirt."

"Invite him up to the lake. I'd love to meet him."

"Did you listen to the whole thing? Did you hear him questioning Houellebecq?"

"Yes. The centre ran it on YouTube in real-time. Take a look: his ebook is online. What a title: *No Reformation*. Bring him, he's your fellow student. We could have a party. He did ask accurate questions, you got to give him that. What's with this writing down questions and submitting them to Dr. Lévy before hand? Never heard of that before."

"Hope you have fun reading his book, Dad. I have to read his devious personality. I'm going home to have a long bath. Talk soon."

Deana sitting in the bathtub of her apartment in Wychwood is trying to wash Mo' out her life. He's untrustworthy and never reveals his cards. Hours later, her father calls.

"Hello Dad. What's up? You peeked at Mo's book?"

"Yeah. Just now got the digital version. *No Reformation* is funny. Funny as hell. I'm reading it. Rénee is reading it. She's laughing her face off. He's been reviewed here and there in small mags—some negative reviews but who cares? These would-be journalists don't get it all. They're complaining about its structure. No Canadian writer is doing what he is doing. Renée thinks it's far-fetched: He seems to be supporting the wrong forces in the world. But I'm not so sure. Haven't finished it. *The National Post*, of all places, gave him a positive review, if you can figure that out."

"Thanks, Dad. I can't figure out Mohammed."

"Deana, Canadian authors don't have his depth. Can you get me a signed copy. Renée would like a signed copy. Mo' has depth. You're a lucky indigenous person to have met him. And, he's an Indian sort of."

"Okay, Dad. I'll invite him. You and mom can enjoy his depth."

7. Love under the Ring Nebula

I GOT TWO kinds of silent stares at the end of the talk: *You-went-too-far look*, and *How-dare-you-come here to Canada with all that confidence?*

Houellebecq and Lévy are on the world stage for a reason: They are hyper-talented at communicating difficult ideas and tolerances within French society. Lévy's intimidating mastery of not only French history but world history and politics, and Houellebecq's expertise in being a shifty presentable author have offered a model for imitation. But what they've taught me is that contemporary acclaimed stars are like well-balanced cosmopolitans; often their bias is so sophisticated and subtle that it's undetectable even by an outsider. Obliquely directed disdain helps get you published in today's commercial presses.

The Bathurst number 7 bus has dropped me off. My phone vibrates against my chest: Deana.

"Mohammed." Long pause.

"You didn't tell me you were a writer. Why not? I was at U of T—Houellebecq and BHL. You were there. My father saw it online. He says you kept your cool engaging France's top intellectuals. He thinks you have a balanced disposition— good grief. Congratulations."

"Congratulations?"

"Yeah, congrats. Why didn't you tell me you were a writer?"

"Did Lévy nominate me for the Nobel? Deana, listen to me: I'm a small-scale novelist without a literary agent, without a publisher, without a homepage even. I didn't tell you because there was nothing to share. You simply can't be annoyed with me. Approximately 1,467 have read my books since 1995, that's 1,467 in 26 years or about 56 people a year. Impressed? Besides, I would have told you, eventually."

"You would have told me? I bet. Want to meet at Bar Neon on Bloor?"

"Are you going to give me shit?"

"Yes."

"Why?"

"You should have told me. Being a writer is important to you. Let's meet there Friday."

"That's at the end of the week," I say.

"Tonight then, eight."

"I know where it is."

"Been there before?"

"Yes."

"Eight."

"Right."

I wear a brand-new white shirt with a button-down collar: that should temper the occasion. Arriving first, I get the best table in the small patio at the back. The outdoor patio and a clear night with a breeze coming off the lake. I order two transparent beers, one for her which I set in her place. She'll appreciate the arrangement. When she looks at the transparent glass of beer, she'll de-stress in a second.

Did my explanation deflate her bad mood? Will she invite me over afterwards? A catchy old dance hit flows out of the patio speakers. Ah, there she is, she's walking toward me. She hears the song. Does she know the lyrics—about a younger man and an older woman? She's looking at me, and lightly dancing to this ancient hit on the way over to me. She's wearing a neon bright yellow T-shirt with a small black stencil of Che Guevara on it. Her fingernails have a neutral sheen. She's wearing a thin, flat gold ring dusted with small Topaz stones. And she's every so slightly made-up.

"You pay the restaurant to play that song?"

"Oh Deana, be nice to me. It's relevant. I'm getting up to kiss you on the cheek, but I think I'll kiss on your lips instead." I kiss her on the lips.

"Hello. You're going to start in on me?"

"How big of a deal would it have been to tell me?" she asks.

Has she forgiven me for not telling her I am an unknown Canadian writer?

In sixty minutes we down two dozen oysters and lots of beer. I've only made three trips to the toilet. Is she counting them? No, I don't think so. I think I'm paranoid. Withholding another secret from her. It'll be a major let-down. She'll know one day. She's content to see me but I can tell she's seething.

"Want to walk me home?"

"Please."

"The beginnings of the Great Square of Pegasus will be visible, you can see Andromeda and some some other DSOs?"

"What?"

"Deep Sky Objects."

"Vega, the alpha star in Lyrae and bunches of nearby stars, I'll show you. You'll have no difficulty seeing their beauty because you're a writer. Lake Rosseau—you're invited. Dad likes you and—he speaks several languages: Mohawk, Cree, Quechua, Arabic—all the languages that are basic to being a Torontonian."

"Azaadi speaks Arabic?"

"What the fuck—how'd you know my father's name?"

"I saw his name on your phone. At Asian Legend, after Cecily Brown. I didn't mean to look. You put your phone face-up on the table."

"He used to be an engineer in Saudi Arabia."

At her place, I see a computer screen which has been hooked up to a telescope. I am beginning to see a pattern. She goes right to the scope and methodically tracks something. Presumably leading her eye to a group of even fainter stars which appear on the screen to be tightly pulled together. The resolution is modest. I see her put in an eyepiece that must weigh nearly a kilo.

"Here, Mohammed. Behold, here's part of the constellation of Lyra."

"Okay, thanks."

I approach the eyepiece. I know how this works. My dark-adapted pupil peers into the 21mm Ethos eyepiece giving me, according to the world wide web, a 1.3 degree True Field of View, praise the heavens. But I wasn't prepared for how her arbitrary composition in the circle-frame thrilled me. Photons at first sight, again. From zillions of years in the past—the spreading evidence of an event that happened just after the invention of Time, and later, the invention of The Elements. The ultra-wide, immersive view blows me away. I know I'm sounding incandescent, but you have to be a bit of an astronomer to appreciate a really good constellation or open cluster or globular or planetary nebulae. A cloud wisp passes, giving a wavy nebulosity to the blazing white, hot alpha star in Lyra; large and small geometric formations beyond belief; mild colour variation after colour variation.

"Deana, I just saw something zip by—an airplane?"

"Fucking satellite. Get used to it. Light pollution = cancer."

"They navigate your self-driving car," I say. I continue looking through the eyepiece. She asks me: "Do you see a very faint small ring that looks like a puff of smoke?"

"Yes, but it's very faint."

"Mo, you're looking at Messier 57, the Ring Nebula—2283 light years away. And you're in Toronto. Not ideal due to a grey sky."

Her hands slowly are moving on my back, and I know soon she's going to tilt my head and kiss me. She's placed her hand on my chest. There's that pattern.

We lie down on her hard bed. The hardness of her bed does not seem like a typical or normal hard. I am guessing it's a hardness that must, undoubtably come, from a knowledge of glossy spa trends in health care.

It all happens even more tenderly than the first time. All the stars in the night sky draw closer. We're relaxing. Then …

Trenchantly, she asks: "Show me your Driver's Licence."

"My Driver's Licence?"

"Yes, your Driver's Licence."

"I brought my passport, just in case you wanted proof of who I really am."

She looks at my passport, and, mollified, hands it back to me.

"Thank you. Let's take a shower," she says tenderly. All her inner fires regarding who I am are extinguished.

With the warm water falling on my back, I kneel on the shower floor and slowly wash her elegant feet. She can't possibly understand the reference. One person's Ordinance of Humility is another's delight.

Our evening ends; I give her a shy, kiss goodbye. She hasn't asked me to stay the night this time.

"Lake Rosseau soon, I'll call you in a while."

The Toronto Transit Commission takes me home.

8. Resection

THE EARTH, NOW furthest from the sun, has spun into summer. It's a complete change of space from my previous cytology exam. What's happening today requires an operating room.

A nurse helps me lie flat on my back. I watch the ceiling roll by as she carefully pushes my gurney into a large elevator, then out into a long hallway with windows that give out to leafy trees. The architects must have considered the calming effect of trees. We glide to a soundless stop outside the O.R. The nurse squeezes my arm reassuringly and goes off down the hall. The section of the hospital has a serious feel to it. The lights are brighter. Hardly anyone talks. And all the staff are wearing similar pastel-coloured scrubs, not the bright colours favoured by junior nurse assistants.

I'm wearing a red gauze head cover, a light blue gown. I look like a brown circus clown in Karachi. The familiar anaesthetist approaches. "Mohammed, how are you feeling? I am not at all sure how much stuff you'll need today and furthermore I don't really know what I'm doing." His assistant smiles and says: "He likes to take risks." Dr. H. Bar must have told these two jokers that I have a sense of humour.

"I ride a bike, a motorbike, sure I like risks," the anaesthetist says.

"Do you have an electric bike? Much faster than those old gasoline bikes."

"I've a Harley Sportster. Love the sound. I drive it for the sound."

"You ride a Harley and you don't know what amount of anaesthetic to give me?"

He smiles and lets my comment pass.

"We're thinking of an epidural. Is that okay with you?"

A South Asian-looking doctor with an English accent is standing beside the other doctors and their assistants. In mid-conversation with the doctors, I ask in, Urdu, if she understands

Urdu. "I understand the language but I get lost speaking it. I was born in Croydon." The crew laughs. I sense no personal rivalries.

"I much prefer a total. Please. Thanks. Please a total. Knock me out totally. It's much easier to pee afterwards."

My bladder-saving surgeon, Dr. H. Bar, arrives. She knows I'm anxious about this procedure. The post-op recovery period is a pain in the dick; there's fear that she might find something that has developed into a tiny mushroom; it may be the cancer has penetrated my bladder wall. To distract me, she proposes a trick I should try with my scientific calculator. Try it in any mode you'll get the same results. We start talking about doing tricks on scientific calculators, but I can't concentrate.

I am wheeled into the operating room with super high ceilings. Dr. H. Bar and her efficient, anonymous assistants move me so I'm directly under the lights. Gently, an assistant puts a plastic tube in my mouth. The ceiling becomes nothing.

She scraped for twenty minutes. I know because the Recovery Room clock indicates this amount of time has gone out of my conscious life. I have to stay overnight. In Ontario, patients are required to stay the night just to make sure they can pee. The hospital wants to avoid having pee-blocked patients returning to emergency. A male nurse with dyed blond hair, who obviously does tons of body-building and has a background accent suggesting Farsi, slowly takes the catheter out of my dick. I realize that I've been hearing Farsi since recovery. Am I in a hospital in Toronto or one in Teheran? I thank the Ayatollahs. Dr. H. Bar is suddenly here. "Mohammed: it was superficial. We'll see you in three months." I feel happy it's over. There are no vultures or eagles overhead. In a few days, I've completely recovered.

9. Muskoka

DEANA TEXTS. She's waiting outside my apartment building. Since a part of Bathurst is closed because of road works, we drive past the house of an old friend, Daoud Heath, who lives on Briar Hill Avenue. He's a photographer whose prints recall some of Robert Frank's as well as works of a few of the great European photographers. Daoud has evolved such a distinctive style that *Time Magazine* commissioned him to do a photo essay on the rising ethnic nationalism in Latvia. "We met at high school years ago."

"That's nice—to live near an old high-school buddy."

"We're close friends. Whenever he and his wife leave town for holidays, he asks me to take out his garbage and recycling bins."

"You're his garbage man?"

"Not really. In fact, Daoud is doing me the favour. The walk to his house and back keeps my blood sugar down. I also water his garden, in the summer. I cut his grass, with a manual mower. This is how a writer makes a living."

"Yeah, right. So you're his handyman?"

"I use his services in return."

"How?"

"As well as being a great photographer, he happens to be a literary editor. Every now and then I ask him to proofread a manuscript I'm working on; it's work, but, *quand on aime, on ne compte pas*."

"Does he suggest endless rewrites?"

"He thinks some passages are over-the-top and will have a negative effect on sales. If he was an acquisitions editor, he'd send me a rejection in two seconds flat."

"He's looking at a manuscript now?"

"Left here on Avenue Road." The conversation fizzles out. She looks in the direction of Daoud's house. Her car, with its made-in-America mind, drives us north on Avenue Road.

"Are we going to try your transparent canoe?"

"Yes we are."

I am slightly nervous about this trip to Lake Rosseau to meet Azaadi and Rénee.

The high-perched eagle-god of geostationary satellites directs us along the 401 to the Barrie exit. Each time the car accelerates to take a small hill in the road, I'm pressed back in my seat. Twenty lanes of multiracial drivers converge on the exit for the historic 400, the highway that will take us to Rosseau. There is such a load of traffic that I can almost see the earth being crushed by the collective weight.

The car changes from collector lanes and places us on the 400. We are being auto-piloted past the flat agricultural Holland Marsh. About an hour later, we pass the cosmopolitan city of Barrie, home to tons of international cuisine, but we don't stop for lunch.

Elon Musk now changes to the High-Occupancy Vehicle lanes. We are surrounded by rolling hills which are filled with deciduous and evergreen trees that have been here for decades but weren't part of the initial growth which was more diverse. She looks at the landscape, not at the road in front of her. This does not make me nervous.

"Are you feeling like an immigrant right here beside these hills, trees and farms?" I ask. "Have you ever driven up the east side of Lake Simcoe? That's super beautiful also, lots of small towns to see."

"Mo,' you're right, those small Ontario towns are nice to look at. The 400 is a white-knuckle drive which I couldn't do without our robot here."

For the last ten minutes, Deana has fallen into a shallow sleep while her hand remains on the steering wheel. I cough, she stirs but continues sleeping. I decide to not wake her and ask myself what does Muskoka mean to me? The day before she came to pick me up I looked up this area which has been part of my life for about fifty years. Muskoka is bounded by Georgian Bay, Haliburton, Simcoe. There's enough water to give everyone in Pakistan an in-ground swimming pool. I sit quietly in the car watching these magical and very familiar old rock formations whiz by.

"Deana, please can we pull over and take a look at these high slabs of granite? I think they want to be acknowledged. I just love these outcrops."

I've succeeded in waking her.

"Sure. I'd like that too."

Carefully, we get out of the car.

"Look at these bore hole lines. That's where they stuffed in dynamite to shatter the rock to make Highway 11.

"Deana, these vertical fields of granite change colour depending on daylight or nightlight, wet or dry or snow or ice, never the same. I've seen icicles 30 metres long filled with sunlight."

Deana and I own this 4.5-billion-year-old pre-Cambrian rock; we own it at least visually. This hard pink material is the core of my identity as a citizen. We get back in the car and are driven over the Severn Bridge. I feel an emotional pinch: Deana and I are now on the vast Canadian Shield. For every college-goer, the Severn marks the end of the flat limestone—the prehistoric seabed of what is now Lake Ontario. I see the sign for Gravenhurst and think about all of humanity, including Mesquas Ukee, all emigrating from Africa, our collective cradle.

"Lunch in Gravenistan?" I ask.

"If you're not dying of hunger, please, I wanted to stop at the best bakery," she says. "It's in Orrville. You'll love it. We take a road with a hilarious name: Tally Ho Swords Road, then we'll be looping around the top back down to Rosseau. Okay with you?"

"Believe it or not I've actually been to the great town of Orrville before."

"Place has the best baker originally from Downsview. My father just loves his bagels. Rénee likes the cheesecake. They have sophisticated coffee also and lunch if you wanted."

"So we are now on a bagel detour, is that right? How could his bagels be better than bagels in my area?"

"His resemble Montreal-bagels. Much better than the NY imitations on Bathurst."

We enter the town of Orrville, population 6,500, fifty percent of Pakistani heritage.

We have precisely made espresso coffee. I take a pee, then carry all the baked goods to the car. Now, she is attentively driving on single lane-size cottage roads which are tunneled by trees.

"Get ready, we're getting closer. Are you nervous?"

"Do I fear your father, you mean? No. Not nervous at all."

The old Edwardian Muskoka of the Old Toronto families has now evolved into a resort area for Toronto's super rich and Americans. Hockey stars live side-by-side with movie stars, though certain Old Toronto families remain. I hear in the near distance the thud thud of a helicopter bringing an executive here from his office in Toronto. The car drives us through another narrow tunnel formed by overhanging tree branches. A true cottage road.

"There any Indian Reserves here?"

"No just a reserve for the professional white class, plus a few Bollywood Indians."

Her father's "cottage" turns out to be a futuristic palace, perhaps the influence of having lived in the Kingdom of Saudi Arabia. We park beside two Teslas; blue jays squawk from the two large-diameter linden trees on either side of the asphalt driveway. We have arrived in Muskoka.

10. Lake Rosseau

THE SO-CALLED COTTAGE is a rectangular block covered with trendy grey steel, and rises so high that I suspect her father had bribed the township council to make an exception to the height restriction bylaw. Somehow, he senses our arrival and opens the door, quickly walks to his daughter, and hugs her. I sense an endless affection between them. "Dad, so this is my math class friend, Mohammed E. Smith." Azaadi Niba'ar, dressed in a white shirt, extends a large bronzed hand, proportioned like Deana's. We shake hands warmly. He's a slim athletic man with shockingly blue eyes. His wife beside him is also handsome.

"Deana has told me all about you. I thought your question at the Lévy-Houellebecq talk was terrific. You sounded like your book. You weren't critical of Israel. Most muslims are automatically critical of it, and they don't look at their own failed states."

"Thank you Azaadi. *No Reformation* took me eighteen years to write. You took the trouble to read it. I'm really touched."

Like its owner, the house is spacious, roughly 30m x 30m with a cathedral ceiling made of oak attached to rust-coloured-steel-inflected modernism. A balcony surrounds a second floor that looks so complex yet coherent it must have been built separately and plonked down by cranes on top of the first floor. Steel beams, wood beams and a large glass roof window which is open to the lake and sky. A chrome oblate spheroid fireplace attached to a long black dark chimney pipe rises up through the second floor and out into the Muskoka air. The fireplace doesn't touch the floor; it's the fashion these days. I wonder if it sways.

Lake Rosseau, now framed by this colossal assertion of a house, looks diminished like a painting. As for the boat house, it's as large as a four-bedroom house and is made of glass on all sides showing off the antique 1920s inboard. I can make out a bed, a closet, and a transparent floor, on steel stilts three metres above the water. "There's where you'll be staying," Azaadi says. "Sleeping over water."

"I have no trouble sleeping on water."

"You've slept on water?"

"Karachi to Liverpool."

"Please stay for as long as you want. Write a book here. There is a perfect room for writing on the second floor. Lake view, *bien sûr*. You're working on something?"

"The next novel. It should have a native character, maybe two or three, who knows?"

"You can put me in it if you want, but I'm hardly typical. Do some research while you're here."

"What's that dome-shaped building near the lake?"

"A solar-powered sauna. Want to try?"

"On such a nice day?"

"Well then, you'll have to come back in the winter when saunas are best although there's nothing wrong with a sauna on a summer's day."

He laughs and, from the side of a thick table made from vertically stacked planks of used and marred pine, hands me a flute filled with a yellowish bubbly liquid. I glance at the spread on the table and notice a 6000ml bottle of Louis Roederer Cristal Champagne. Is he expecting people to join us? A party?

"You've come to the right place to write a book. Appropriate everything you want. I've appropriated a few myself. Not Urdu, mind you. Haven't appropriated that yet. Could happen. Urdu. A salad language. My first language has relatively fewer words but you can improvise endless combinations of verbs to suit what comes along. They are called holophrases."

"Long live the languages," I say lifting a glass. I should have said long live the smaller languages, but that would have been considered churlish.

I can't place his accent geographically. It's different from Deana's. It has a very faint trace of Arabic. "Research? Here's some: I use Indigenous Development Grants from Ottawa. Invest the profits to fund left-wing movements here and there. Give some to indigenous folks in Peru and India to pay for land claim litigation. I'm a hemispheric Robin Hood. I rob from Ottawa with its non-existent development policy to save indigenous communities in the third world. This is true research. I forgot to add I have an account in Nevis—15 to 20% return. Don't forget to mention that."

"I noticed the chopper."

"I bought it during the mid-eighties when the prices were depressed; now it's worth about seven left-wing liberation armies in Latin America."

His wife sidles into our conversation, a laptop tugged close to her chest, smiling.

"This is Renée. I got my blue eyes by just being near her for more than two decades." Renée extends her hand. A grip like a steelworker. She is a spitting image of Boy George.

"Mohammed, pleasure to meet you. Azaadi thinks he has the freedom to go on and on. Just ask him to be quiet if he doesn't stop. You had lunch? Please help yourself." She says glancing at the table. Her deep mellifluous voice delightfully floats into my ear. I see a field of several cheeses at room temperature.

"Now, Mohammed, we've been sensitive about what you may or may not like to eat. We don't have any pork in the house."

"But, I love pork. Azaadi, did you know your name means freedom in Urdu?"

"Okay then, I do have some pork in the house," she says.

Deana always drinks Chardonnay and/or transparent beer. Her dad has cracked open a bottle of Marcassin Estate. He's thrilled to see his daughter. She walks to her room to change and freshen up, and now since she came back she's been emitting light from bright black and yellow leggings and a 3D T-shirt of the constellation Orion. She's sitting on the sofa, Lake Rosseau disappearing in the distance behind her as background. I leave Azaadi and walk over to her with a cool glass of Chardonnay. I'm surprised to see her knitting.

"Knitting?"

"Yes, I do it while I drive. A pair of socks." She's relaxing as a result of being near Azaadi.

"You're connecting with your father well."

"Like Electra the daughter of King Agamemnon and Queen Clytemnestra, you think?"

"Who? Deana, I am unable to keep up with your mind."

She looks down over her astronomy T-shirt and says: "Mohammed, the star Betelgeuse is over what part of my tit? Apparent magnitude -3.0, 3600 Kelvin."

She's sprawled out on the large black divan, texting, surfing, whatever. I hope she'll come down to the boat house later tonight. It was beautiful sleeping with her at her place near St. Clair Street. Does she have a telescope here too?

Back to chat with Azaadi. Another monologue emerges for no reason. "I left the First Nation, U of T engineering, worked in Saudi Arabia as an oil engineer, then came back and met Renée. Anyway, I'm so glad to meet you. I know you like paintings, want to see my Ellen Redlake paintings? She's an indigenous artist. I've got two new ones by her. Brand new. You saw the show at the AGO, but you probably liked Cecily Brown more because she's white? Deana's biological mother was from Oslo."

"Dad, stop brow-beating Mohammed."

"Okay, let's consider the paintings."

Azaadi steers me to a family recreation room. Now I can get a wide view of Lake Rosseau. The sun is at its zenith, almost deliberately its light falls on Redlake's bright paintings.

"Do we have to have these family line discussions? I mean Mohammed has just arrived here," Rénee says.

"Have a smoke before we look? I've stocks in two pot companies: *Groups of Seven*, and another brand called Snow *Blind Treaty*, both marketed by the provincial government Cannabis stores country-wide."

We vape up. The light-yellow coloured bubbles are making me giddy. "The brand names get you in any trouble?"

"No trouble. No trouble at all. Indigenous people enjoy my sense of humour; they love it."

Fearfully I say: "I didn't mean to imply natives don't have a sense of humour."

"Indigenous People do have a sense of humour. I can make you laugh right at this moment. Here's a laugh: I'll nominate you to be the first Pakistani-Canadian head of The Assembly of First Nations. Basically, you're an Indian but from over there."

"I'd like that job very much. The pay good?" I ask.

From the black leather divan, Deana in a raised voice says: "Dad. Don't bug Mohammed. He's my friend. Be nice."

"Azaadi, be nice to Mohammed," Rénee says. "He's your daughter's friend. Listen to Deana."

Father and daughter laugh. Her laughter carries across the gymnasium-size living room. I look up at the second floor made of steel and recycled wood. Douglas fir-like wood planks set into the bolted talons of steel beams which have been allowed to rust to a brown orange high cultural standard and then covered in a glossy urethane. I should open my mind to the stereotypes, then move beyond them. Yes, like everyone, I do carry some mild inexcusable racist stereotypes of Indigenous People. It's impossible not to, because equity-seeking groups say these stereotypes are logged in the unconscious I am now beginning to think that Canada has a vast diversity of Natives, some who are so rich that they would never pronounce the word *reparations*, and others who drink unboiled water and get ill, and a few who helicoptered up to bourgeois modernity without the CBC noticing it. I should no longer think that natives are always anti-colonial and blocking roads for unrequited land treaties. They should be … I stop myself on the word "They". This "They" sets me against the natives and makes me a racist. Azaadi has passed me a loaded vaporizer. I feel welcomed into the post-colonial world of financially complex Canadian natives. My racism toward natives faces extinction.

"Please, am I smoking? *Groups of Seven*? Or *Snow Blind Treaty*?" He still hasn't answered. He's busy vaping, now exhaling smoke rings in the shape of teepees. "Azaadi, I never supposed you'd be so talented." He still doesn't answer my question.

Deana is getting loaded on one of her father's brands of marijuana. I inhale and exhale the stuff, casting a light blue fog to flow across Lake Rosseau which has become a disintegrated object made out of water surrounded by trees, and bird songs. The lake has lost its identity in the cycle of life, death and rebirth. I have another sip. I get higher and higher, like a native eagle flying in circles of freedom. Had Azaadi really given me *Snow Blind Treaty*? He answers. "*Snow*. Not sure if I gave you *Snow*, Islamic brother Mohammed. I've forgotten. Does it matter? You look stoned as shit. Go look in the mirror. Both are good. We need to come up with a new name for a brand of pot. I'll give you some unceded Treaty territory in payment." I hesitate. *Treaty* is hitting me big time. I'm like totally losing my shit. Never thought *Snow* could get me this damn high, higher than what I can get from government pot shops in Toronto. Hell with government pot. Am I a Blue Jay? I'm high in Azaadi's chopper above Lake Rosseau. His pot is ruining my computational biology, *et cetera*. I'm still thinking about a brand name! I've got a brand name: *Bedrooms of the Nation*.

"The generation we're trying to get addicted to this stuff won't get the reference to Lester Pearson." With a slow, outstretched hand he guides me to the still, calm eastern wall of this large square house which is so high that I could see domesticated eagles perched on the red cedar rafters.

I keep looking at Azaadi and wondering about his sun tan. Somehow, he's accessed my mind; the Snow Blind Treaty has made my mind readable to him. "I got it when I was south on business."

"I think it was Pierre Elliot Trudeau who was in the bedrooms of the nation," I say.

"My tan."

"How'd you know I was thinking of asking you? Never mind. You'll condemn me as racist if I tell you some natives can read minds."

"Natives can see inside the minds of white people only, but only if we're standing near Hemlock. Do you accept this? Didn't think so. You're definitely a certifiable Bear-Spirit hater. We are going to send you to the Peterborough Petroglyphs to be shamed by a tour guide for all to see."

Deana says: "Dad, you totally forgot about the paintings. If you're going talk about Redlake's paintings I'm coming over." Her bare feet, still clean from my washing of them, tuck back into sandals. "Wait. Renée is coming. We're all coming to see the new paintings." Renée, wearing baggy silk pantaloons, looks at the works.

"I know all the exact clothes in the paintings," she says. Totally stonedhenged.

Azaadi is on a roll. "Karachi or Sriracha?"

"Lahore. We did live in Karachi, Sriracha made my stomach ache," I say.

"Where I was in Saudi, there was a man called Abdul, from Sriracha. He managed our residential compound. Abdul introduced me to Lebanese Muhammara. He said he was from a small town, Clarkabad, outside Lahore." Azaadi imitates Abdul's accent better than I could. Azaadi has become Abdul: "Go Lahore Government College to study economics. I passed. I not brilliant, but pass. I make application to leave Pakistan. I arrive ten years ago. In Saudi immigration I saying I am not Maharashtriyan psychomusicologist from Chiang Mai. So they accept me. The compound owner has progressive daughter who is lesbian. He accept. No issue. Father educated Bristol chemistry department where lesbians are common. He studied genetic chemistry. She study at University of Toronto. No one in family worries. University of Toronto. Don't mention but I think she was reject other places. Saudi is like Canada, we have tons of snow rooms for skiing. We have snow park in Riyadh. Daughter might to become citizen. Canadian citizen. I go back Lahore for holidays to read holy scriptures in sacerdotal language. Bloody hell."

Tears of joy are falling down Deana's face. She blasts *San Francisco* by the Village People on the cottage stereo, which costs thousands. We are all swaying to this song. We are all drunk, stoned and swaying to music from the homo erotic 80s. Azaadi says: "Deana, we are talking, can you turn it down? Please." Deana laughs, she and Renée are dancing. Deana conforms. "Okay Dad. I'll turn it down soon."

"Abdul sounds like a nice man with a sense of humour like yours. He Christian? Did you become friends? Do I really remind you of Abdul?"

"Not to be seeing Abdul in you, Jinnab. He come from minority. Christian, yes," Azaadi says. Perhaps due to *Groups of Seven* and the alcohol, Azaadi is now trapped in Abdul's syntax. The Urdu syntax won't leave him. Good. He can't seem to break out of the colonial prison of Abdul's accent. "Abdul taking me to a large shopping mall in the Riyadh Gallery Mall, King Fahd Rd, King Fahd, 262, Riyadh 12262, Saudi Arabia. We walk around the wide halls which are much bigger than Yorkdale or even bigger than Badshahi Mosque. And Yorkdale does not to have aquariums with fish so large it looks like a permanent Damien Hirst exhibition, except the large fish in this Mall move slowly but not as slowly as in a Hirst piece: the formaldehyde is stopping the fish from moving in his fish tank sculptural works. Saudi men—all in white robes and in a religious formaldehyde—look at the fish. Daydreaming. Arts expression."

"Did Abdul really mention Damien Hirst?"

Azaadi ignores my question—he has become Abdul. "I take you to a restaurant, right here. Guess name? What called? Guess Mr Azaadi. To guess please. Restaurant in Riyadh? Name? Called simply: Lebanese Restaurant. Boring name. But low IQ arabs get it. Restaurant is Lebanese."

The Sriracha accent has left the native ex-chief and flown to the red cedar rafters to join the eagle. "In Saudi, we ate exactly what I would have eaten in Toronto. The meat tastes better due to Islam, but only slightly. At the Lebanese Restaurant in Riyadh they serve Muhammara. The Lebanese restaurants in Toronto have better Muhammara than in Saudi. And guess what, Mohammed?"

"What?"

"Along with the *Foie Gras directement de Paris* we have *Muhammara directement de Toronto.* How's that for internationalism? Are your racist stereotypes dying yet?"

I face the facts: I am now friends with a native woman who lives in Paris and the south of France in the summers, likes 1950s Girl Groups, likes Basmati rice, Korean food and whose father has a helicopter with a landing pad, and they make tons of anti-native jokes. I must be stoned. My brain particle interaction spreadsheets are so shit stoned that they have stopped taking data.

"Yes my racism is dying in my mind. Azaadi. Dying forever, like forever. Deana, you feeling that internationalism?"

Deana is standing near. Her arms keep rustling against mine. She says: "See, where I got my love and respect for pre-colonial cuisine? From my beloved Dad." Azaadi looks at Deana, confirming a bond that goes beyond love-of-the-land and mining rights.

"Azaadi, how many acres are you giving me for *Bedrooms of the Nation*?"

"I spoke with forked tongue."

We turn toward Redlake's paintings. The first one, Azaadi tells us, is called *Aunty Numinous Number One*. Strange and unreasonable as a title. "The most expensive painting done by a Native: six million Canadian dollars. Far less than the white painters," he says indifferently. "Here in Muskoka we had a written alphabet that pre-dates the Chinese alphabet by 10,000 years. Whitey destroyed all the evidence. Chinese are Muskokans. They know it. We know it. In the period of the Great Muskoka Culture, some tribes walked west across the Bering Ice Cap before the Russian bear spirit invented Cyrillic. They wrote the G5 code in Muskochinese. *Wall Street Journal*. Check. Not kidding. Code written on snake skin. Deana knows. I'll show you later. You'll see and respect."

"Azaadi, with due anti-racist ecology—I mean apology—the *Groups of Seven* pot might be clouding your judgment."

He ignores me. Like an art restorer, he moves close to the painting, starting to concentrate on the pigments. We follow Azaadi into the pigments. Then, when Azaadi pulls back to take in the entire painting, we collectively, like a tribe, pull back to view the image in all its nativist glory. We move as art critics whisked into one. We stand next to a vast image made on Italian linen stretched over an oak frame measuring at least 4 by 3 metres. Azaadi touches the canvas and says: "Tight as a shaman's bum."

The labyrinthine painting not so much hangs on the wall but feels magnetically suspended out from the wall which is, floor to ceiling, made of utterly un-sanded long planks of spruce, 2" x 12" x 10'. The painting has fifty images of Cardinals locked on the oil paint, feathers drenched in linseed oil, fluttering and panicking across the bands of chroma. The anti-bourgeois architectural values in the wall become apparent when I notice that some planks are warped out of the horizontal plane by 2 to 5 cm or more. This warping is repeated across the huge side of this Saudi palace to cause a satisfying beauty, like a granite shore meeting a frozen, white lake. February in Canada. Jesus Mac Jesus, I'm stoned to the tomahawk. We're inside the leading edge of lake-side architecture, standing in a room, 20m x 20m, a vaulting ceiling with native eagles flying in and out of the clouds of smoke from the *Group of Seven*. Has he given us LSD? This visual experience is not pot induced, in my opinion.

Azaadi presses the edge of one of the protruding planks and the 3 x 2 metres south-facing glass doors slide open. Heavenly, pine-scented air flows in along with waves of Keith and Tex singing *Stop that train*. Azaadi acknowledges the party sounds from across the lake. "Speaking about local folk, you should meet Eddy Longwetsky, a systematic native from Lake of Bays who loves to plant wild rice in front of the cottages of actors from Hollywood. The wild rice clogs up the waterfront. Hollywooders can't swim, their electric motorboats and electric jet skis get tangled in native rights to hunt and farm freely. They can't stop him. Then he harvests the wild rice and sells it to the rich liberals, even the Hollywood liberals."

"Can you buy Eddy Longwetsky's rice at the Rosseau Farmer's market?"

"No choice, I have to. Nice guy. Stuck in 1970. But, as you know, Deana and I love Basmati rice. Wild rice is crunchy stuff for the native birds of Canada. Loons make their nest from the stems. Eddy makes the packages from recycled paper; on the front, he puts a drawing of a native woman wearing a jingle dress and a head of feathers." Azaadi holds up a package:

RICE À ROSSEAU
ORGANIC WILD RICE FROM
YOUR OWN FRONT YARD
500 GRAMS   RK

"University-educated postcolonials protested the Aunty Jemima on the package. Doesn't stop him. He says he's a feminist, so it's okay to do this. Increases sales. He has his contradictions."

"I protested also but Eddy *would* not listen to me," Rénee says.

"You didn't protest loudly enough. Eddy *would* listen to you," Azaadi says.

"Azaadi, what should I have done? Burn my bra at Lake Rosseau?"

"Too extreme, given the cultural standards up here."

"Mum, don't talk like that. Far too radical. Besides, I really like the packaging on his wild rice."

Now, slowly, the world that Redlake has painted, in conjunction either with the *Snow Blind Treaty* or *Bedrooms of the Nation*, or *Groups of Seven*, and the description of the wild rice package, is causing me to appreciate the current postcolonial rice situation Eddy Longwetsky has created. Indigenous suffering swirls out of the paintings. I'm stoned shitless and feeling a deep cultural shock. I can handle it. I am protected by a priesthood of Great Blue Herons.

We're gazing at the painting. Against the dominant colour is a vibrating steel grey-black with major First Nations figures holding hands with Canadian celebrities. They lie horizontally in a circle, I guess a cosmic circle. Leonard Cohen is holding hands with

Tecumseh who is holding hands with Sitting Bull who is holding hands with tribal Shipibo holding hands with Adivasi who are holding hands with Burton Cummings. Who is holding hands with Leonard Cohen? He is holding hands with a clan mother who is holding hands with Gordon Lightfoot. Redlake has a hyper internationalized way of painting. The other iconographic change goes like this: All the Indigenous People, painted à la Max Beckman, are wearing western clothing from decades ago. Idiosyncratic. Ever so slightly. They're all wearing moccasins like in the Québécois TV show, *Mohawk Girls*. Beads are pulled out centrifugally, but Renée, with a Boy George understanding of clothing, blurts out: "That woman chief is wearing a short skirt—Dior's 1953 Palmyre, a short evening dress, in *rayonne acétate de cellulose*, and her bag, which is whizzing outward, is a Louis Vuitton Speedy hand bag made world-wide famous by Audrey Hepburn and her depicted native look-a-like. And, the hat—the hat is by Ferdinand Le Grand, and the clan mother is wearing one Crocodile skin shoe handmade by Caovilla." And then she explains apologetically: "I used to do costumes for a theatre company."

Enough. We step out on the lake-front patio. On the right, wooden steps take us down to the lake. We inhale Muskoka air. You can't get clean air in China or India. Deana and Renée move off to the side and sit down in Muskoka chairs, drinks nearby. Uncannily, Renée is too much for my imagination. I'm praying that Azaadi will not be able to access Boy George in my mind. Despite *Stop that train* pulsing across the lake, I can't get *Karma Chameleon* out of my mind which is now governed by *Snow Blind Treaty*.

Azaadi and I walk down the steps. "I did like your book but I don't think you understand colonialism. Liberals like class struggle issues so long as they're in a far-away place. Class struggle issues too close to home makes liberals become conservative. I keep hearing *Karma Chameleon* coming off you so one of these nights I'll put a dream-vision into your mind. It will be nearly frightening but you'll wake up well-rested." He pulls out his cellphone: *Karma Chameleon* fills the lake.

11. Crescent Moon over Muskoka

WE'RE SITTING IN Muskoka chairs basking in the early afternoon sunlight. Renée's hands are manicured beyond perfection.

"Mo,' why don't you ask Deana to try her new canoe?"

"Let's do it. I'll show you my special place where I go to be alone," Deana says.

At the dock, she's takes off her T-shirt and leggings before tilting the canoe into the lake. She enters it on one leg like a dancer.

"See how I'm walking down the centre of the canoe?"

"Stoned, slightly drunk and careful. What about life jackets?"

"Don't worry."

"I'm serious. What about water safety? I'm hydrophobic."

"Nothing to fear."

She's tip-toed along the glass bottom and is now sitting at the bow of the canoe, paddle in hand.

"You're driving."

"Why? You know the lake?"

I sit in the stern and paddle out and back along the shallows nearer the shore. It's hard to stop looking at the bottom of the lake, moving under the canoe. Those two dark shapes are a pair of sleeping Bass. Their waving tails reflect sunlight as we drift over them. Her transparent canoe has made the lake into a floating aquarium.

"Mo', pull us closer into the shoreline, near those overhanging trees." I look through the bottom of the canoe and see an underworld of milfoil. Deana gracefully reaches into the water, uproots some and tosses them in the canoe. "Milfoil. It's clogging up parts of the lake. Hard to grow wild rice, let alone go to Port Carling and buy gin."

"Doesn't wild rice clog up the lake?"

Deana silently takes in the surroundings.

The lake reflects a bright, nearly cloudless sky. A woodpecker drills methodically into a tree. The one sign of effort offsets the overall feeling of peace.

"See that little sand beach? Set in there? This is where I come to be alone."

It's more of a mudflat than a sandy beach, but the canoe nudges in, as if it's glad to be here. A small channel of open water through the bullrushes indicates a stream emptying into the lake, with lily pads guarded by frogs. The quiet quack of a duck. A blue dragonfly hovers over Deana.

"Sometimes I feel I'm the spirit of this estuary," Deana says. "I am a goddess. I guard its fertility."

"Deana, you're still high."

Years ago, I was a camp counsellor at Camp Boulderwood—a Muskoka summer camp for inner-city kids. There, I learned to canoe. I perform an expert wide J-stroke, turning the canoe toward the beach. I try to build up enough courage to tell her but I'm distracted by the setting: an intelligent astronomer in a silver bikini who likes me; the smell of pine needles, patches of emerald green moss on the rising rock shore. Shadows ripple over her shoulders, her hair gleaming in the sunlight.

I'm the dark interloper who has fallen in love with her. The see-through hull of the canoe is made from an oil by-product: Azaadi, shareholder in a dying gasoline industry whose profits he pours into left-wing indigenous resistance movements, indirectly contributed to the manufacture of this canoe. We disembark. The act of standing up reminds my bladder to empty itself.

"I need to take a leak."

"I just told you this place is special, and your reaction is to urinate on it."

"Sorry, I have to. We've been drinking."

"I brought you here so we could feel purity of this place. Now you're going to pee." She's not joking. Has she gone native like Peter O'Toole in *Lawerence of Arabia*?

Colonialism aside, there is no solution to this predicament, the hydraulic pressure is building so I head behind the green growth and start to pee. To my side, deposited on a rock, is a long snake skin. She's come up behind me when I'm peeing—too intimate. Her hand moves on my back. She sees my red urine falling on juvenile leafy fronds.

"Mo'. You're peeing blood. Are you okay?"

"Fine. I'm fine."

"You're bleeding."

"Hematuria. Normal. You made me do all the paddling." I remember some applicable latin and try to make light of my red piss: "Deana, my bladder speaks latin to me: *Nullius addictus iurare in verba magistri*. It's sworn to not let me master it."

"Sure, I am impressed. Cut the latin crap. Tell the truth. What's the matter with you?"

The trickle stops, I turn to her.

"Bladder cancer. They can fix with Aspirin if it's taken during a full moon."

"Why didn't you tell me before?"

"It's curable."

"Seriously, Mo, why the secret?"

This can't be easy for her: She must feel that she wasn't given a choice when we were intimate. She doesn't pull away, but I feel a wall rising up between us. I'm suddenly feeling my age. And her age.

"We'll talk later. Did you see the snake skin?"

"I see a snake skin, did you see it?" she asks.

"Yes, I saw it. You're not picking it up are you?"

She puts her arms around me and says: "An Ancient native person, Asclepius, tells us that snakes shed their skin to revive and heal themselves."

"Really?"

The stress of keeping my affliction private causes me to pull into the safety of a daydream. She is going to leave me. Crisis provokes a daydream, like in urology. I'm hearing Johnny Rivers singing *The Snake*. While researching astronomy, I discovered that in 1963 many advances were made in astronomy: New Zealand mathematician Roy Kerr found the exact solution to Einstein's field equations, and in the very same year—1963—civil-rights activist Oscar Brown wrote *The Snake*.

She's being light-spirited about this, but I think she's offended. She must think I duped her somehow. I've duped her again.

"Rasalhague is the head of the doctor in the constellation of Ophiuchus. This ancient doctor in the night sky above Lake Rosseau brought a dead snake back to life by using a plant. The plant contained medicinal power. You'll be cured because we're going to smoke non-government grass under the constellations of Serpens Caput and Serpens Cauda—it's the name for the tail of the serpent."

"Deana, this will save me?"

"But you never know, myth is a kind of science. Science one day, myth the next. I really got carried away."

"You think you got carried away? In my head, I was just listening to that famous Johnny Rivers song *The Snake*."

"Johnny Rivers? Never heard of him."

Despite her compassionate exterior, her mood has darkened.

A short-term daydream flits by, leaving a deposit of nonsense: Did native cosmologists make Newtonian telescopes with a focal ratio of 4.7 and large diameter mirrors from polished white Muskoka granite, coated with Aluminum & Silicon Dioxide and ground pine needles, surrounded by a cylinder of black turkey vulture feathers glued together with honey and bear gut? Did they use stacked pumpernickel bagels and sun-dried eyes of a Golden Eagle to make an eyepiece? Did they buy the bagels from Schindler's Bagels on Bathurst? Did their white granite, honey and feather telescopes reveal the Hulse–Taylor binary pulsar PSR 1913+16 in the constellation of Aquila? Based on her hobby and wanting to continue having informed chats with her, I've been reading about pulsars. According to Indigenous astronomers, zero smoke signals were returned from this area of space. This thought is racist. But slowly, I am coming to terms with my racism. Most people who immigrate to Canada are suspicious of natives; some, like me were racist. I try to delete this daydream from my mind in case she can read minds like her father.

"Mohammed, is there anything else?"

"No other secrets. You know all there is to know about me: writer with curable cancer, modest income, not a settler."

"I'll make you into a non-settler. Do have any kids I don't know about? Tell the fucking truth."

"I'm telling the truth. Nothing but the truth from now on. I've got the name for a Pakistani restaurant right in that super upscale town we drove through."

"What are you talking about, Mo'?"

"I am talking about creating Mus-koftas and Musko-naans right here in Muskoka."

"They sound good to me," she says.

"By the way, you mentioned Greek and Arabic words."

"Greeks and Arabs got them from Indigenous People in Babylon. Not Babylon, NY. Let's canoe up the little stream."

We get back in the canoe and glide along a small stream as it narrows to just twice the width of the canoe. The stream is thick with water lilies. A bullfrog eyes me judgmentally. I have committed a moral trespass in Deana's sanctuary. I'm privileged to be seeing something that only a few select people can see: lilies on the surface of a small stream in a part of Ontario where one can't hear the small explosions inside cylinders of internal combustion engines. The weeds push at the canoe—we are no longer on water but moving on a carpet of water-soaked vegetation. The moral bullfrog leaps off a lily pad and into the fecund water.

A current pushes the canoe close to some bullrushes. A skein of ducks launches and skims the glassy water. Mergansers. We head out of the stream and back into the lake. Under the canoe the single-tone greenish depth, bars of sunshine disappear into blackness. Will there ever be time in my life when I'll stop visiting my surgeon? A reply arrives: *Beloved Mohammed, you'll never stop seeing your surgeon. No matter what the South Asian Indians say in their prayers to Rasalhague, the star of bladder cancer, only scientifically minded Jews can save you.*

Her father's house appears about 300 metres in front of the canoe.

"Can we practice exponents?"

"Practice exponents? In the middle of the lake?"

"We're not in the middle of the lake, are we?"

"Your father's house sits on that Precambrian rock which has been there for: four-times-ten-to-the-power-of-nine years.

"You brought your calculator? You're weird. 4 billion years."

"What's with the flag on Azaadi's flag pole? Could it be …?" The breeze causes it to unfurl. "My god, it's the flag of Pakistan."

"Dad is flying it in your honour."

"You arrange that?"

We paddle proudly home. When we arrive we can see from the dock that Azaadi and Renée are having a red drink. He holds out two glasses of Karkade for us. Has Azaadi sensed our exponents practice? I suppose that his telepathy can't see my thought hundreds of metres away, but he's full of surprises.

"Some *Foie gras*? Mohammed, just out of idle curiosity, why do you have your calculator in your hand, when you're canoeing?"

"He was counting birds, so many of them up here. Azaadi, will you stop bugging Mohammed?" Renée asserts diplomatically.

After dinner, Deana kisses us all Good Night, and she recedes into her bedroom. The three of us have grappa, then Azaadi walks me down to my open-concept space over the boat house with its ceiling window. The floor is transparent plexiglass. The motor boat looks small down there.

"If you get up early enough, you'll be able to see the morning mist through the glass floor—first you're walking on clouds then you start to see the water below you. Sleep well. See you in the morning."

I get undressed and lie down on the bed, half covered under a cotton sheet. The window is open. Through the screen a cool night breeze off the lake rustles down my chest. The voice of a 70 million year old loon rises and fades. I turn off the bedside light. My pupils dilate to 5.5mm. I can see fields of stars through the ceiling window. The loon's cry pulses up to the heavens and then falls back toward me in the form of French Horns holding a pleasant octave. Azaadi's place brings about visions.

Deana's fingers used to comb my argentine chest hairs. She hasn't wandered down to see me. A wee bit of colour in the pee has scared her off. What if Dr. H. Bar sees zero evidence of more cancer? This is likely given all the drugs they've used on me. Did Deana want someone perfectly healthy, with 20-20 vision and a blood sugar of less than 5.5mmol/L? Such a big deal over something that can be cured by Aspirin, lemons, steel-cut oats, mangoes, and a few words in a strange sacred language: Remission: *Inshallah*, remission.

12. Healing

INVISIBLE BIRDS SING all around me. Their songs blend into the early morning sunlight to become one single chorus of magnificence.

I get out of bed, walk on the cold glass floor and see the lake below my naked feet. I slip on my Birkenstocks. Jesus, it's a beautiful morning. I feel happy to be here, but fear the coming loneliness.

A pair of black Peshawari chappals look out of place on a shelf near the floor. Abdul, Azaadi's compound manager in Saudi Arabia, must have given them to him when he left. They're authentic, well-crafted Pakistani-made chappals with an engraved galactic spiral just like the colonial Brogues I still wear to celebrate anti-colonialism. A note in balloonish handwriting states: *Mohammed, a little gift from your homeland, Azaadi.* I toss off the German sandals and slip my feet into the chappals. Peshawar is a city in Northern Pakistan which despite everything has an openly gay culture.

His gift uplifts me. He's made me into a Pakistani walking on the waters of Muskoka. Maybe she'll come tonight. Yesterday, she seemed to accept my health issue, but her early departure from dinner was ominous.

I put on my new black shoes, grey shorts with zip-pockets, and a fresh white T-shirt and walk under the Pakistani flag to the cottage. I open the massive patio door and say: "Good morning Azaadi, Renée, Deana. Everyone sleep well?"

"Well indeed," Azaadi responds.

"Mohammed, please have some breakfast," Renée says. I help myself to Basturma and scrambled eggs, and some Besan-ki-roti with coriander, Armenian sausage, and chapatis made from chickpea flour. So much inter-cultural connection.

I sit at the table and join them. Deana is looking moody.

"I've told Dad and Renée about your cancer."

The word cancer hits me in the face. The Armenian omelette and roti is stuck in my throat. I take a sip of coffee to buy time, and say: "I should have told you. Forgive me. I was dishonest."

Azaadi's eyes light up with a smile: He admires my sincere apology. "Deana, Mohammed wasn't being dishonest, at least not intentionally. These things go into remission—it's the name of the game. I know many people who have gone into remission."

"Dad, you said that you'd offer Mohammed a wilderness healing session. Before we head back to Toronto."

"Truth be told, it's Renée's idea. I called Eddy after you told us. So this afternoon we're going to heal him. Indigenous medicine will turn Mohammed into a raccoon for 220 moons. Eddy says he thinks he knows how to do it."

"He looked it up online to see how's it done?" Renée asks cheerfully.

"I remember enough to start us off," Azaadi says. "I mean it's only bladder cancer which is fixable. Eddy Longwetsky. Nature's handyman. He can fix anything."

"Dad, it's cancer. Not a fucking leg cramp."

"Azaadi, how on earth is Eddy going to help?" Renée asks. "All he knows how to do is grow rice on people's lakes and fly his planes."

"He's more connected with the communities, than I am. Not to worry, my friends, we're going to shrink his cancer to the size of one Kalonji seed. Less than that. We are going to fix this, don't worry. Mohammed, have another coffee. Eddy'll be here in one hour. He's never late. Here, take a look at my old *National Geographic* magazines. It's a chilly morning, let's light a fire."

Deana, Renée and I clutter away all the breakfast plates, cups and saucers. From across the gymnasium I hear: "Those Peshawari chappals look natural on him. Shalwar Kameez next time. When the doorbell rings, let Eddy in okay? Though he'll probably just come in without knocking, like northern folk. I also got him a pair of those shoes Mo' is wearing: Amazon.ca. I'm not kidding. You can buy all of Pakistan including the military generals on Amazon.ca. He'll be wearing them today, I can promise you. Eddy lives in them."

We're sitting on leather armchairs around the hanging fireplace. Presumably in preparation for the healing, Azaadi has turned on the sound system.

"Mohammed, do you dig the Modern Jazz Quartet? Here's *Love Me, Pretty Baby*."

"Not sure I've heard of them. Do you think it's chilly in here because the air-conditioning is on?" I ask.

"Azaadi, he's right. The AC is on. Who left it on?" Renée asks.

"This Muskoka real-estate magazine is filled with modern-looking crap houses. Dad, the AC is on automatic."

"I like our design more. Especially the roof patio. Last night, I set up my astrophotography telescope, Stellina, on the top floor. The captures are excellent. I saw everything." Deana passes her iPhone around to share her astrophotography.

"Are the stars in any way going to help Mohammed?" Azaadi asks.

"Yes, they will. Especially Electra in the Pleiades. But too bad for Mo', we can't see them in the summer."

The Modern Jazz Quartet is patently modern; then, suddenly, I hear a few bars from the *Moonlight Sonata*—their door bell.

"Mohammed, please let Eddy in." He's behaving as if the healing is a formal occasion. I quickly get up and walk toward the door.

"I'm sure you're going to like Eddy," Renée says. "I can feel it."

I open the door. So this is Eddy Longwetsky. A lean, tall, sun-tanned man with large beautifully manicured nails, cowboy boots, skin-tight grey Lululemon-looking pants and a pressed blue half-sleeved shirt. Nature's gentleman. His blue eyes are amplified by the shirt.

"Brother Mohammed. *Salaam alaikum*. Deana has told me all about you. Welcome to Muskoka."

"Wa 'alaykumu s-salam. Brother Eddy, Please come in."

Eddy strolls in as he's perfectly at home and sits with his back to the lake. In seconds, I'm absolutely relaxed with him, and I don't know why.

To make conversation, Azaadi says: "Eddy, I've told our Mohammed about your rice-growing. He's impressed. Knows all about rice."

"I don't have much experience with growing rice," I say. "Wild rice is something new to me."

"We are getting current with Basmati. I've got plans. I'll go India and have a look at the suppliers. Want to come with me? We'll bring back some seeds. These cottagers—all bourgeois types—they don't know about the health benefits of wild rice. They think it's for ducks. Azaadi here doesn't identify with it."

"Eddy, count me among those types. I haven't any clue how to cook it. Also, I should tell you that the High Commission of India in Ottawa will not give me a visa, so I can't come with you. But I'll be with you in spirit. Remember to not drink the water, and ask the waiters to open the water bottle in front of you."

Not even a smile from Deana. Nothing is going to shift her moodiness. Her bronze body could have been beside mine last night. We could have heard the loons together.

"As regardin' health issues, Mo' excuse me for being direct, but Azaadi, told me about what the issue is. I hope you're okay with two Indigenous whack-jobs tampering with your bladder energies."

"As long as there aren't any insertions, I'm fine with whatever you do." Finally, Deana laughs.

"Eddy can heal anything," Renée says.

"Renée, are you high?" Azaadi says. "That online stuff can't be taken seriously. But we haven't a choice. We gotta do something. We have Eddy, and I remember that once someone had headaches 24/7. Eddy put him in a shed. Windows shut. Doors shut. Full moon. Ed gave him nothing but carrots for two days. He never had a headache again. There was a bunch of stuff—people dancing, wolves running, speaking in tongues, but that was just theatre. And all this was before the internet. Eddy will invent a healing. Bladders are the mothers of invention."

"Looks like Mohammed's in good hands," Deana says. Perhaps her spirits are lifting and forgiveness is around the corner. After I'm healed maybe she'll swallow my papillary urothelial neoplasm like she did the first time. Can she contract anything from me? Utterly impossible. But she's not looking at me as she usually does. She hasn't come near me to brush her arm against mine at all. She's wearing a white shirt like the ones she used to wear during math class.

Looking toward Renée, Eddy says: "We need some makeup, lipstick, concealer, foundation. And mascara and primer and some blusher and lip stuff. And can I have some breakfast first?"

"Holy birchbark. How do you know make-up products?" Renée asks.

"This healing is Azaadi's idea," Eddy says. "So he's got to put on the makeup. And, according to traditional knowledge we can't take any mirrors."

"Why in heaven would we take mirrors? Eddy. Listen. You have to put on make-up too. Why should you stay make-up free? Do phones count as mirrors?"

"I don't remember any of this shit," Eddy says. "Whitey made it all up, And put it on YouTube and have to follow it cause there is nothin else."

Renée leaves to get the healing supplies.

"No make-up for Mo'?" Deana asks. Her mood might be lifting.

"Mo' absolutely has to have make-up," Azaadi says. "And maybe this healing will speed up my own pee flow. Two birds, one stoned session. Check-list time: large pot for the Ayahuasca, *Psychotria viridis* and some puking buckets, unless the forest spirits won't let us puke on the forest floor. How do we heat the water? For the plant? I'm not lighting fires."

"Where'd you get that Ayahuasca? Isn't it a Controlled Substance?" I ask.

"Got it up the lake from these Hollywood Muskoka people," Eddy says. "Some are so depressed that they have to do it year round. Only a matter of time before Jeff Bezos or Elon Musk makes pills for Third World spiritualism. That'll save them. Back then it was beaver tails, now it's hallucinogenics. Fair trade."

"Those are vision drugs. Jesus. Hey Mo' you got a brand name for Jeff Bezos's Ayahuasca?" Azaadi asks.

"Dad, you live up here, you're friends with some of them."

"Friends with who? Deana, tell me?"

"Last summer at the General Store I saw you chatting with Justin Timberlake."

"He's a singer, not a Hollywood actor."

"Azaadi, can't think of a name for Ayahuasca pills," I say.

"We're not healing until you come up with a brand name."

"Okay, what about. *Bladderkoka*?"

"Mo', you're a super talented writer, but *Bedrooms of the nation* was over the top," Renée points out.

Azaadi produces a piece of paper from his shirt pocket in his expansive manner. "Friends, here's our check-list: a pot, water for the *Psychotria viridis*, a bag for all the make-up, and an iPad for the music. I've selected a song to play when we get loaded. No women allowed. Sorry. Is there place to plug in a kettle? Yes, I got it—we can plug it to the boat."

"I know how to make a fire. I lived in England. Please, let's not forget to pack some marijuana," I say.

"Yes, take something familiar," Renée says. "I've rolled a few *Bedrooms*. Mo', don't be nervous. This is your healing."

"Mohammed, this will be your very own personal *Reformation*," Azaadi says.

"The men got to a have sauna first," Eddy says.

"Why?" Azaadi asks.

"Cleansing purposes. We can't smell human. It offends the spirits. Also, if we raise our body temperatures, we enhance our spirit-bodies. The sauna works like traditional community stuff—the temp shoots up."

"A sauna in the glass dome," I say.

"The girls will be able to see us from the patio—but who gives a fuck? You're not white so you're Indigenous. Mohammed: I'm inducting you into your new tribe," Eddy says, starting to sound business-like.

"What new tribe?" Azaadi asks.

"Yes, what new tribe?" I ask.

"He's just pulling your leg," Azaadi says. "You'll get to know Eddy, he's like that. He'll induct you into the Ice-Age original Muskokasauna tribe for thirty minutes."

"This is a transparent solar-powered sauna which makes steam with energy provided by the Sun Spirit," Eddy says. "We're going to sweat up a storm."

The large glass dome smells of Eucalyptus. The photosensitive elements that are layered into the glass are transparent. We'll be in the nude and clearly visible from the Saudi cottage.

"We're going to be naked. Deana and Renée are already looking at us. I'm not shy: must be the Islam in my bones."

"Forget them, Mo'. They won't be able to see nothin' We'll be in our spirit forms."

"I built the sauna for twenty people to sit in a circle. During winter evenings, it's heavenly to come for a Muskokasauna. Minus 20C outside. Unique place. I'll voice in the temperature, and how long do you want to stay in the heat, Mohammed? It's your healing, you decide. We thought thirty minutes might fix your bladder?"

"Fifteen should do it," I say.

"I'll set if for twenty-five minutes at 47C. Hot, but we'll give it our best."

"You think he can handle it, Azaadi?"

"I'll try," I say.

"Deana and Renée are vanishing due to the rising steam. Why are they laughing?"

"Mohammed, please open that picnic basket to your left," Eddy says. "I've brought some *Kibbeh Nayyeh*. Nothing like a little raw Lebanese meat when it's 46C and rising."

"You said we didn't want to carry any offensive smells."

"Shit, let's eat it anyway."

I collect the world around me. I'm in a sauna with two Europeanized Canadian Indigenous People who like Basturma, Basmati rice and roti. I have Aspirin-curable cancer, I was banging his daughter—and—her father actually appreciated that fact, and now Eddy and Azaadi are my best friends in the universe, and we're all eating raw meat.

"Shit Eddy, you forgot to take off your cowboy boots. That's why the girls were laughing. Eddy. Buddy, you're in the nude with cowboy boots on. You should have worn those sandals."

The heat is moving right into my bones, expanding them to neanderthal scales. My lungs are burning. A laser projects the time and temperature onto the undulating steam: 45C, 19 minutes remaining. Our skins are going red. The sauna is converting us into hemispheric Indians.

"This is a bit painful," I say.

"What a wimp. Azaadi, hold the course. Don't turn'er down. Right now, his bladder is more important than his body. Keep it going."

"I'm just a spirit, with a bladder."

Rain issues from my body and eddies into the marble floor which is, anyway you look at it, a metamorphic rock recrystallized carbonate-limestone.

"I'm sweating onto your marble floor. Sorry. By the way, Azaadi, that flag you put up for me, it was an Algerian flag, not the flag of Pakistan. Good of you to think of me."

"No problem. Don't worry about the marble, it's marble from Carrara, and I don't remember accurately exactly where, but the construction people told me it was from Lunigiana. Your sweat is at home here."

I'm being cleansed for the curing that will take place on the island. Eddy is beside me. I feel loved. These two are attempting to help me. Finally, I feel fully integrated into Canada because of the love I feel from these men. Gradually, the temperature falls as well as the steam. From the dome we see Deana and Renée, standing waist high in mist. We wrap towels around our waists and walk down to the boat house and load everything into the antique inboard with varnished wood panels.

"Nobody putting on life jackets?" I ask.

"Life? Jackets? Are you kidding?" Azaadi says. "We were just cleansed—we can't put that plastic shit near us, and Mohammed, listen to me: life jackets are a form of colonialism."

Captain Azaadi starts the motor and puts the 8-metre boat into reverse. He's seen my mind flash metric for a moment, I'm certain. Eddy sits in a state of luxurious ease at the back of the boat, his arms spread across the seat.

"This is a vintage 1929 Ditchburn Viking. Chrysler Crown Engine 8 cylinders. The Toronto Harbour Police had a few of these as high-speed pursuit vessels. But I'll go slow."

"I feel as secure as a cancer victim in an ambulance. Azaadi, your sauna looks like Haram al Sharif. Why are we doing this?"

"We're doing this to keep the girls happy. Go with the flow, Mohammed. Yeah, I went there and loved it. But everyone thought I was a secret agent. East Jerusalem, no sweet grass."

He turns a key. Eight pistons under the deck quietly thud. The boat shakes with vibration. Then the twin exhaust in the stern, just above water level cough and gurgle. Let the healing begin.

"Why didn't you get a new electric boat?" I boldly ask.

"Muskoka in the 1920s—there's no sound like it. It's music to the ears. Like the sound of a Harley."

Renée and Deana wave goodbye from the shore. The gasoline from the stern exhaust ports gets in my lungs. I knew Azaadi would push the throttle forward all the way. The black needles swing merrily across the five white dials. The boat arches up steady as a rocket. Our waves splash against the shoreline, making the seagulls take flight. The boat moves south. I'm totally caught up in the feel and sound of the inboard. Eventually, we pull into a small island which is four billion years old. No one lives here. We unload everything from the boat.

"Just a few trees and us. Azaadi chose it." Eddy says.

"I'll gather some stones for a fireplace. And get some wood," I say. The island silent.

"And, friends," Eddy says, "here's the pot for the water. We'll drink this stuff within the hour. Get ready."

Time passes. Azaadi and Eddy say nothing. They have gone inward, becoming part of the island's silence. After a while, we boil the mix, drink it, and start puking on pine needles of the island floor. A Great Blue Heron flies down to eat masticated Armenian sausages and eggs. We lie down and tolerate the stomach cramps under a transparent tarp that Eddy, moving like a ballerina among the tree branches, has hung.

We repeat the drinking and puking cycle as we're supposed to, but no vision emerges. Then, I feel relief settling into my mind. I've never felt relief like this before. Birds approach in inquisitive steps, then fly away, then approach again and gaze at us. The afternoon spins into a moonless dark, starry, evening.

We put more wood on the embers and smoke *Bedrooms*, which makes us multi-hemispherically stoned. Eddy and Azaadi are going to blow smoke onto my crotch but not smoke from marijuana. I can't think of what sort of smoke they've decided to blow. I trust them. Healing is the ultimate in developing a friendship.

Azaadi pulls a shaman's drum from out of the boat's storage compartment, and sets one end of it between his heels. He quickly taps his thumbs on the Corning Gorilla Glass screen of his phone. Muddy Waters is singing *Forty Days and Forty Nights*. The shaman drum connects with the Chicago Blues, and I see African-American men in powder blue Cadillacs driving through Muskoka. Then comes the magical blues harp solo riding on an upbeat three chord, 12 bar blues. I hear the voice of the blues harp address me directly:

"Mohammed, that's Little Walter playing the harp for your healing. Can you dig it?"

"I can dig it."

The music chosen for my healing is appropriate: the lyrics connect with my current life. It's been forty days and forty nights since a woman left a man; the weather has been great but now it's raining and he misses her and needs her badly. It almost feels like I've been alone on this island in the middle of Muskoka for 40 nights and 40 days.

Am I seeing pink stars? "The dimethyltryptamine is doing its thing," Azaadi says, now walking around bewildered looking.

"Azaadi, calm down and sit," Eddy says. "We got to choose our animals."

"Okay, Eddy, time for *Bedrooms*," I say.

We smoke. More stars shine in the night sky. Azaadi from within his knapsack takes out a piece of braided sweet grass.

"Eddy, please light me up. It's time to fix the old bladder, all the braids are made from mathematical native knowledge."

"Here we go, *click click* … and we have red embers and some nice smoke."

Azaadi waves the red embers at the tip of the grass over the crotch of my shorts. They take turns blowing sweet grass smoke over my bladder.

The grass has been braided with three strands representing mind, body, and dimethyltryptamine which is making me experience general dilation.

"Azaadi, do you have any idea what you're doing?"

"Mohammed, when Indians braid this grass, they use the seven strands representing the seven knowledge keepers."

"The magic power of nature's pure math," I say.

The carpet of brown pine needles comforts me. Eons of pine trees have shed their leaves here. We're in the period of healing. I've become part of the international equity-seeking recombination of tribes. *Allah-o-Akbar*. I see a bird flying in the sky, its wings flapping, but the creature makes no progress in any direction due to being trapped in my mind.

An electric hurricane lamp thuds light onto our faces. We start looking into each other's eyes. Harmony sets in. Again, wave after wave of friendship hits me.

I see or imagine a spinning ball made out of twigs. Every few seconds, a single feather flies off the ball and up into the trees. A feather flies off. Azaadi has lost control. We climb further into the drug. And, now suddenly, I have the illusion I can peer into Azaadi's mind.

Eddy' s voice through the smoke:

"Choose your totemic animal, Mohammed. It can be a bird or a reptile if you want, but remember after you select it you're not allowed to kill this creature. It will be your guide through life."

"Okay, I think I'll take the Blue Heron up there in the constellation of Cygnus, the Blue Heron."

"Kinda suits you," Eddy says.

I can't repress what I'm hearing in Azaadi's mind. Visions are the cement of friendship. I can feel that he'd do anything so his daughter will connect with me again.

I hear a conversation between him and Renée:

Azaadi's voice: *"I think you changed very fundamentally. How fundamentally? You were taking more and more pills."*

Renée's voice: *"I have to tell you something. I'll soon be shapeshifting to become what I've always wanted to be. A woman. A woman in the physical sense."*

Azaadi's voice: *"I love you even if you're a man or a woman, or a duck. It's your spirit being I love. That can take any form."*

"Azaadi, are you ok? I'm seeing images of you talking with some man."

He ignores my question. I continue seeing him talking with—it's now clear—René, not Renée. She's become a man, as she perhaps was initially. I try to stop seeing Azaadi's vision.

Eddy's says: "We're choosing our animal guides. Looks like he chose Renée instead." Eddy begins banging the shaman's drum to summon his own animal.

"Something isn't right here," he says.

It's Azaadi. He's coming out of his trance. "What isn't right is that Mo' accessed my vision? Also, this idea we can choose our spirit helpers, where did you get that from, Eddy? Is it true?"

"It's true."

"How do you know it's true?"

"Internet."

"Isn't it the other way around? Aren't the animals supposed to come in a vision and choose us?"

"Naw. Anyways, it worked like I said, didn't it? You chose Renée."

"I didn't experience a Heron," I say. The argument is going nowhere. Besides, Azaadi plainly needs counselling.

"Azaadi, how is all this going to help my bladder cancer?"

"Let whitey fix it, Mo'. This healing isn't working out. Eddy must have done something in the wrong order. But anyway, we bonded as good friends. I can see that my daughter loves the shit out of you. I'm beginning to love you too. I want my daughter connected with an august, cosmopolitan man from the ancient city of Lahore. Mohammed, we need you in our family. I'll never forget how you handled those two dudes from France. You were fearless. No true Canadian would have done that."

"Azaadi, why not sit down here?"

He's sweating profusely. He pauses to catch his breath, but the vision reclaims him.

"Hello. Renée, what are you doing at this healing?"

"Azaadi, Renée is not here. She's back at the cottage," Eddy says.

Eddy, with his shiny black cowboy boots beside him, is sitting on a stump looking into the fire. I can see pine needles in between his toes: It looks like he's enjoying the ticklish feeling.

We all fall into our private reveries. I think we've fallen asleep. I wake up and notice that Azaadi is lying face up beside me. Azaadi looks white.

"Would it help if you told me what you saw?"

Azaadi stares up with blue eyes glazed over.

"He must have seen somethin, real bad."

The voice of Azaadi from far away, the distant side of a trance.

They did something to the dorsal nerve bundle. It is used to carry the sensation from my penis...

Azaadi is speaking in Renée's voice.

"The glands and the urethra which carries urine were separated from the main shaft of my penis. Then they cut off the corpora cavernosa …"

"Holy shit that ain't no vision. That's somethin else." Eddy feels instinctively for his crotch to see if it's still there.

"Do you know how they gave me my clitoris? They hacked the head off my penis like a tree in a forest. Then they attached what was left to the genitals. Fine stitchwork. Now, do you want to hear how they made my vagina …?"

Eddy puts his hands over his ears.

"They made it out of the leftover penis. The stump they didn't hack off is used to make a real functional or nearly functional clitoris. They cut off my balls for student surgeons to…"

Eddy is throwing up in the forest.

"I got two psychological approvals. I had to get these approvals to get the transition operation done."

Renée's voice concludes proudly.

Now I know how Boy George came into my ears earlier on. They surgically added an "e" to René's name. Did that alter Rénee's tribal affiliation, I wonder? Is she now a full-blooded Inca and from the same Peruvian civilization as Azaadi? Though he claims Muskokaian origin—more or less. Could that have happened in the operating room? Tribal shapeshifting. I went along with the vision, and got wrapped up in all that cold and bloody flesh dangling off the operating table. Apparently, this kind of operation is covered in Iran by the government. And, without countless psychiatric exams. The global cha-cha-cha of people changing so much, so quickly, and so permanently was doing me in.

At around midnight Azaadi comes to his senses. We walk down to the boat, holding onto each other like shell-shocked soldiers returning from a pointless battle. Azaadi tells me to drive us back. I bring the engine to life, the noisy pistons, and smelly fumes almost make me puke again. I can't see a thing it's so dark. I consider following a few major stars back to the boathouse … the boathouse where I'll be sleeping for one more night. Alone.

Azaadi was able to talk again in his own voice as soon as we touched the dock.

"Mohammad, that stuff hit me hard. I feel as though you could see my mind."

"Azaadi, Eddy, I feel cured. I peed yellow back there. On the island. I used a flashlight, but in my excitement, I accidentally pissed on it, hope it's still working. Thank you both. What about the make-up? Why did we take it if we didn't use it?"

"Mohammed, use your phone. Take a look at yourself. Renée and Deana will love it."

We walk up to the cottage.

"Mo, why are you the only one wearing make-up?" Rénee asks.

"I don't know why—these two took advantage of me."

"According to the info we got from the web, only Azaadi was supposed to paint his own face," she says.

"Rénee, I don't know what happened."

"Mo', you look funny, there's perfect symmetry to the lines," Deana says. "Dad and Eddy—really unfair to do that to Mo'."

They all continue looking at my face. Finally, Deana offers me some remover. Quickly, their copy of an ancient mask on my face vanishes into a 3-Ply Kleenex. But she doesn't come too close to me. We drive back the next day after lunch. Despite the healing she leaves me.

13. Freezing

CINDY, SALIMAH, ZOE or Musafareen: I wonder which nurse will help me get ready for my routine cystoscopy. Recently, nurses had given me Bacillus Calmette-Guerin (BCG) treatments. This intravesical immunotherapy for treating early-stage bladder cancer has failed. BCG put me in a non-stop peeing festival, with a bit of pain at every peeing event. When I met friends in cafés, they would wonder why I went to the bathroom so often, sometimes without mentioning it. I've developed an ability to memorize five-digit bathroom door codes that Toronto cafés use to keep their loos private. People with bladders that are not working at the normal flush rate get treated differently by friends.

During my Montreal era, I had dinner one evening, with friends at L'Express. This is a brightly lit, noisy French restaurant on rue Saint-Denis, where the waiters are friendly and serve wine at 18 degrees Celsius. I ordered Salade de betteraves en vinaigrette et de roquette and fish-and-chips followed by Ile Flottante au caramel. The beets were delicious. It was a noisy dinner with a famous Canadian-Lebanese writer and a few visual artists. We were sitting at a window table.

No one at the table knows I have cancer. I go to the YMCA many times a week where I walk on rolling black carpets, silently lift light weights, and swim length after length. I eat more vegetables than meat, so why me?

The noise of knives and forks reminds me of metal surgical instruments that will be going inside me for as long as I live. Every three months, I have intimate contact with metal. Eventually, all my friends at this table and all the waiters in this restaurant will one day have metal inside their bodies. Friends: Metal will become part of your anatomy. Take a look at a series of imaginary x-ray photographs in the sequential style of Eadweard Muybridge. Here we're early apes walking on all fours at approximately the same time as the birth of the Lambda Orionis Cluster—a mere five million years old. Centuries later, we've become upright individuals marching out of Africa, all the way to Saint Clair Avenue and Christie Street, metal in our bones.

Years ago, Dr. H. Bar suggested Mitomycin with EDMA. An electronic catheter is inserted; electronic patches are stuck to my groin, these help the electrons move in my bladder. The anti-cancer particles spin at nearly the speed of light and they stay in my bladder for 30 minutes making me glow red from my groin. With EDMA, the post-electron unit-area pressure is so great that one could go into low orbit due to bladder pressure. My bladder is getting Canadian health care, the best public health care in the world after France.

Into the waiting area, clipboard in hand, Musafareen calls out "Mohammed E. Smith". It's my turn. Musafareen is looking after me today. I think she's from Addis Ababa or somewhere nearby. She's wearing blue scrubs, lighter blue gloves, red Adidas running shoes. She assigns a locker for me. I take off my clothes, put on paper-thin socks, a blue gown and sign the pre-surgical consent forms. She asks: "Any allergies?" I say: "No. Nothing to worry about I'm not allergic to anything except dogs, cats and horses."

"We haven't seen any horses here," Musafareen says.

"I know, there are no horses here. Just in case a horse comes galloping along when Dr. Helena Bar is up there with her camera."

"Don't worry at all. That most likely will not happen."

She directs me to the metal table. I lie down face up, feet in stirrups with the gown lifted up to my waist. The sterilization equipment is right next to my balls. My scrotum, now the size of a black hole, has migrated up to my throat.

"I'm just going to clean and freeze you."

Is the liquid from Addis Ababa, I consider asking but instead ask: "Where are you going for your holidays?"

"We'll be driving to North Carolina for a beach vacation. I'm taking my daughters. Are you going anywhere?"

I'm going to Bladderistan for a few weeks of rest on yellow beaches, I feel like saying but don't.

"Oh, I might go to Muskoka for a short holiday."

Will Dr. H. Bar see any tiny flapping butterflies in my bladder? The beginnings of mild panic are making me do thought experiments. Dr. H. Bar walks in. My lips are dry. I am here with the lights above me and the colour monitor to my side. Within a few minutes, on the monitor beside me, I'll see a wide-angle view of the walls of my urethra emerge. It's a fleshy voyage with a small dark hole at the end, and then the great hall of my bladder. The introspection is modern, real, and can be made poetic if I can remove the panic, but sometimes I can't. The metal cystoscopy table has me in a lithotomy position. Panic behind me, panic in me. Panic in front of me.

The nurse did not say: "Get in the lithotomy position." I had to look that up. Knees in the air, legs wide apart, so that my dick and balls are prepped in the sterile fashion. A liquid from Djibouti, or Asmara, or Mogadishu is expertly fed into my dick which freezes but does not become brittle. I feel her gloved, alcohol-cooled hands on my dick. The Lidocaine topical goes into the head of my knob and travels down the pee tract becoming Antarctica.

I'm feeling sorry for myself. Will it hurt? Yes, it will. The cystoscopy lasts about five minutes. I admire the way her confident, well-proportioned hands guide the camera.

My mind wanders into my hippocampus with my heart beating like the heart of a hummingbird—260 beats per minute. Outside, in the waiting area, there are endless lines of bleeding bladders waiting for the zapping laser sting to *dust* the cancer.

Fear has taught me how to stay calm. I am losing it today. It's not the pain but the possibility she'll see something that requires further exploration. Sometimes, I'm as calm as a lubricated cucumber, sometimes, all the metal, mirrors and the scintillating monitor, instead of scaring the living fucking shit out of me, distract me. I don't lose it in front of the nurse or Dr. H. Bar. In front of them, I show a sense of guillotine humour. Just think how much Azaadi would admire me if he could see me taking that metal snake inside me. I wish I could sit in his classic motor boat and ride all over Lake Rosseau.

Will the dick-freezing last until she's finished the cystoscopy? It's good for up to an hour of frozen dick. Will my dick suddenly de-freeze sending pain signals to my hippo-whatever-campus? I've had catheters in me over 50 times. Every three months, metal becomes my new best friend. I can feel another thought experiment coming. I wish this was not happening to me again and again, but was happening instead to Trump, Netanyahu, Duterte, Valadimir Putin. Margaret Thatcher should get posthumous *snake-and-lens*, while Indira Gandhi and Gandhi both get rusty-infection-causing catheters. May these people lie collectively in a cold necrocaththerpolis, their tombstones made from bent and twisted old rusty catheters. Does Imran Khan get a necrocatheter? Fidel Castro—Fidel has been inducted into the Canadian Hall of Ultra Progressive Bladders.

I think of Rénée's subtle sense of humour and caring. I think tons about Azaadi's affection for me. I never felt judged by them. Just thinking about Muskoka saves me.

Will I die from bladder cancer if I don't come here every three months? Will it go away on its own? The answers are as clear as the heliopause. The routine temporary pain caused by the camera and laser eyes are part of my new life. There will be pain. Mohammed, face it: There will be battles in the ditches of your bladder cancer.

My salvation connects with the brightly coloured fall leaves. These fallen things resemble what she sees inside me. I think of the swirling leaves and don't think of the high-tech medical commodities around me just now. Then, I hear words from paradise. It's Dr. H. Bar saying: "Mohammed, I'm coming out now." The war is over. Over for three months. The colour monitor shows the thing retracing its earlier voyage into my bladder and out of my canal. Dr. H. Bar pulls out the camera which stares at bladders all day long. Has this camera developed prosopagnosia due to saving bladder after bladder?

14. Missing Deana

I'M YOUTUBING VERSIONS of Roy Orbison's *Only the Lonely*. This helps me to cry my face off but really I should thermalize my tears by putting my head in the oven. I lied to her about being a writer, I hid my bladder from her, so no news from Deana since we went up to Azaadi and Renée's. I crave smelling her scent of sunshine on dry moss.

I can't make any progress on my manuscript: I have writer's block.

I'm thinking about days, afternoons, and evenings in her high-rise corner apartment in upscale Toronto. She has a 270 degree vaulting view of the Toronto sky, and a spacious balcony. We've seen sunsets and constellations together; she introduced me to her two telescopes which she treated as living extensions of her eyes. She has one Tele Vue-85 and a huge 15" reflector made by *Obsession Telescopes*. Until they are taken up to Muskoka for summer and fall, they both live out on her balcony under super-sealed plastic coverings. This mirror, like the mirrors on the James Webb Space Telescope, loves the cold.

She showed me how to calculate the *speed* of a particular telescope by dividing focal length of the tube by the diameter of the clear aperture. Then we would make love. Then she shows me how to find out the *True Field of View* of a 21 mm *Ethos* eyepiece which has a *Field Stop* of 36.2 mm:

$(36.2 \text{ mm} / 1520 \text{ mm}) (360° / 2\pi) = 1.3°$—which is a view as large as three moons across in the sky.

She does all numbers in her head. Then she'd cook something indigenous to Uttar Pradesh while I lounged on her couch watching CNN.

When the moon was experiencing earthshine, or when it was full, she, being a matured amateur astronomer, would smoothly mention all the Latin names of the seas: *Mare Anguis*—Serpent Sea; *Mare Cognitum*—Sea That Has Become Known. When she got to *Mare Humorum* she moved her hand to my back; this led indirectly to *Mare Vaporum* which lead directly to *Mare Nectaris*. But alas, I digress into the *Lacus Solitudinis*—the sea we can't see. Wake up Mohammed: She's left you—let the tears flow into *Lacus Lacrimae*.

I remember one afternoon, in bed she started to squeeze me tightly.

"Deana: you've increased your squeeze, I can hardly breathe."

"It's a special time to be holding you."

"I feel special beside you Deana, but I need to breathe."

"Squeezing harder and harder. Mo' 19 years ago John Herrington—Chickasaw Nation—was in space. He's up there in spirit right above us. Want me to show you on my phone?"

"Herrington? Who? Check on your phone?"

I look at her phone.

"What are you talking about?"

"I mean in a few months' time we'll celebrate the First Native American in space. He docked with the Space Shuttle Endeavour."

"Was he allowed to take traditional head dress up into orbit?"

"You're going to stop being a racist pig, aren't you? He took up his nation's flag."

"The American Flag? Why did you need to take a high school maths course? You did those numbers in your head."

"Not the Stars and Stripes. I need to take an astrophysics course and needed to brush up. And I met you."

Herrington beat racism to airy thinness by becoming a human celestial object causing a memorable conjunction between me and her. And now she's not here. Little events like this haunt me. The tears drip from my eyes like *Orion's Sword*, one little emission nebula after another. I've become the *The Crying Man Nebula*.

I remember a moonless night at her place when the *seeing* was excellent. *Seeing* is a word that astronomers use when the sky is transparent. She was happily cooking when suddenly her apartment became black—a metropolis-wide power failure. From across her kitchen, she threw the cooking spoon in the sink and dashed for her telescope. The apartment was plunged into darkness. I can't see the large poster of the famous 1968 photo *Earthrise*; us—all of us humans—spinning through space on a round top. From her balcony we watch as streets, one by one fall into an sub-equatorial African blackness.

"Yippie. This will be as good a *seeing* as when we went to Benguerra Island—Bortle Class 2 skies—very black."

"Where's Benguerra Island? What's caused this city-wide black out?" I ask.

"China," she says.

Within thirty minutes, our pupils dilate. The leaves rustle in the two oak trees below, dogs bark like they do in any Third World city after nightfall. The Milky Way surges with field stars: long streams of dotted ribbons sprayed across the Toronto black-out. It's like she's lives for a blackout. The Milky Way is like a line of white coke on black glass. With the photons from major things up there reflecting in her eyes, she passes me her 2 x 54 Ultra-wide binoculars so I can connect the starry dots in the constellations. I had fallen in love with her during the blackout.

"Deana, you look super happy. But this power outage means your fridge will defrost all the salmon and deer. And we won't get to eat that *Bún Thịt Nướng* you were cooking. I, Mohammed E. Smith from the city of Lahore, love grilled pork and rice noodles."

"I've another feast for you. Quick, help me set up the large telescope. And, tell your pupils to dilate more now. I know yours won't dilate as much as mine because you're old—I mean older." Older, yes, bladder cancer yes, keep silent, yes. Shut the fuck up and look at the beautiful stars yes, watch the rotation of barred galaxies: Keep your secrets and lose Deana—that's what you've done. *Jusqu'ici tout va bien.*

"Why do you like me so much if my pupils don't dilate?"

She puts her arms around me and kisses me until my pupils are fully dilated. She sets the telescope to Polaris—the centre of things from the Earth's point of view, for the next 26,000 years or so. She guides the time machine, I peer over the edge of the telescope into the tube: the demonic mirror in the base is gathering light from the stars. Looking through the eye piece she says: "Even though it's the wrong time of the year, magically I've found Aldebaran the alpha star in Taurus. I can see the Hyades and now I'm slewing up to the Pleiades, Messier 45—the Seven Sisters—almost but not quite in the field of view—Mo' you ready?" After a long look, she moves away from the eyepiece, brushing her lips over my cheek and kissing me.

"Most of the star names are in Urdu. You should like that."

"*Ab initio*—I fear ethnic nationalism, even up there. Do you think that the population of Toronto will increase after this blackout?"

I look into the 2 inch eyepiece. Its brand name, written in green letters, is *Ethos*. In the circle field, she's has composed stars with a formal rigour. The stars appear to sing to each other using music written on sheets of dusty nebulosity. The nearly black background, the bright stars surrounded by what she calls dust lanes, shock me. I stare into the eyepiece for ages. I adjust the focuser while my other hand touches her back.

"Deana, why are the stars wiggling and not twinkling?"

"Ground convection currents. Toronto losing its hot air."

I had forgotten about my cancer until she shows me the Orion Nebula which looks like the inside of my modestly clusterfucked bladder. Looking at this star nursery I get visually intoxicated; therefore, I can't tell her about my cancer, not now, not when the moment is right in front of me. She might get angry if I tell her or worse, she might feel sorry for me. She could say why did you sleep with me without giving me the option to say no due to your illness. My precession of character makes me hate myself.

Looking up from *Ethos* I ask: "Deana, how do I pronounce Pleiades?" She reaches into my shirt and touches my nipples and says: "Play-with-dees, like this Mohammed."

"Be serious." I'm crying due to the beauty of Pleiades.

She kisses the tears moving down the front of my face. During various nights, under her tutelage, I've seen: The Seven Sisters—an open cluster, 444.2 light years away, M45.

In her other telescope, a refractor we see things slightly differently. "You are now seeing them through through calcium fluorite crystal glass—made from the material that comes from stars. Strange isn't?"

Now, due directly to my lying, she's $4.20^{(15)}$ kilometers away. She saw my bladder, rich with papillary clusters. The red in my pee contains iron, the iron and everything else we are made from comes directly from up there. My cancer has blasted her far away into post-$LGBTQ^{(2)}$ Muskoka, safe with her loving father, Renée, Lake Rosseau and the Great Blue Herons.

I turn on the lights in my apartment after sitting in the dark for hours. I look at my bookshelf. I look at my phone. No reply to my imaginary text? Mohammed, are you nuts? Irrational? You never had a rational period in your life? Mohammed: No one, not even Donald Trump, replies to imaginary texts. Only intellectuals in Wuhan do that. I'm here alone, the first quarter moon's terminator shows me the craters of urban loneliness. I've been terminated. I see Indigenous People getting ready to land near *Mare Australe*, the first set of oxygen-tight metal teepees are on the moon—anti-racist comments like that would make her laugh.

Under her guidance the constellations shifted smoothly across the sky, now they murmurate erratically changing direction.

We plant Amaryllis bulbs which, strangely, bloomed during the middle of our summer romance. She liked kissing over the buds. Deana and the case for Native Logic: Kissing in front the flowers makes them grow into larger flowers. Was she suffering from confirmation bias? I can see her laughing. She was many things and slightly off-beat; this is what made falling in love so easy. And she's super rich which makes her even more attractive. Sweet Jesus of Lahore, bring her back to me.

To keep things in working order, occasionally I see a woman who invites me to her place. I lie to her also. This person is really a distraction from Deana. She's a psychologist who works in a progressive drug rehab programme based on the Portuguese model which she believes in. I met her online. She doesn't know enough about high-end, low-circulation literature, so no point mentioning my complex books to her. I didn't tell her I'm a writer. I see a pattern.

I enter Distraction's apartment. With her bare foot, she closes the doors. A kiss becomes unstoppable. She reaches down to her own crotch—oh, Jesus, I can now feel an Azaadi-inflicted flash-back. An airy disk filled with a transparent vision of me at the island, that day after breakfast. A flash-back due to *Bedrooms of the Nation* hitting my system, I can smell the sweet quantum particles of grass smoke being waved over my balls. Distraction is holding her erect penis in front of me. She's a woman who owns a dick? Hello. It's Toronto, anything is possible. Azaadi please stop it. For post-colonialism's sake, stop it. Your daughter is not interested in me—I'm an ill liar. I really want her, but Azaadi, she's gone. I really want to come to your cottage for the rest of my life. I want to use her Stellina astrophotography telescope, but brother Azaadi, what to do?

Azaadi is trying to stop me from cheating on his daughter by projecting dream sequences in my head. Is he sending me messages from his Tesla parked outside my apartment building? I open my curtains. Only a black Ford, possibly filled with gasoline. I can't see him but he must be nearby. I try to tele-communicate with Azaadi: *Brother Azaadi, seeing this woman does not count for me. Distraction, strictly. Your daughter is the only one that counts. Keep your mental stuff at Lake Rosseau. Keep it off me. Please.* He's heard me: This woman's penis changes into something familiar. She's drawing me into her utterly new sexuality: male superimposed over female, female superimposed over male and all reproduction or breeder state-transitions in between. I don't know what I've just fucked, but it could have been a proper woman that Germaine Greer would have liked.

Please, Roy Orbison, save me. I have to keep Distraction out of my social circle in case Deana returns. Azaadi, brother, if you can hear me: The loneliness is making me into a proper time-pass-pisswallah. At home, I watch a 1967 Brazilian film, *Terre en trance* by Glauber Rocha; I watch the entire film, nothing else to do. I watch Satyajit Ray's 1955 *Pather Panchali*. I toast a sesame bagel which helps chase away the sadness. I face the chronological fact that I'll be alone at this age. I'm an older man, a goof really, who has fallen in love with a younger woman who thinks she's invincible to the usual health chronology that we are all subjected to.

Deana and I used to walk along Grenadier Pond in High Park, and watch the young ducklings become full-throated distinct males and distinct females with distinctly no in between sexualities—but who knows what scientific claims we'll read next.

We saw Shakespeare in the Park. The actors in *Hamlet* are males and females. The park does not stage *Coriolanus*. I attempt to impress Deana by mentioning other plays all the way to *Waiting for Godot*, and making educated comments and reciting lines like, *First Citizen … If the wars eat us not up, they will; and there's all the love they bear us*. And, of course, *The fault, dear Brutus, is not in our stars, But in ourselves.*

"Mo', you have such a memory for Euro-settler-trivia. I'd like to give all the Euro-settlers a guaranteed income—you heard it here first."

We walk hand in hand in Toronto's beautiful parks. Sherwood Ravine, Cedervale Ravine, Humber—Rouge Park has too much traffic noise coming from the 401—we'd hear half as much noise if everyone drove electric cars, theoretically, I mean a better signal to noise ratio.

The courage to text her builds: Hello. Miss you. What South Asian thing are you cooking err, being colonized by, I mean? Can I come for dinner? Silence. I give up. Zero replies attributable directly to my fibs. But, why should I disclose my cancer? That's my business. Usually, girlfriends leave for the usual reasons: Cancer is a form of adultery; you can't mention it or they'll leave you.

Deana, excuse the non-indigenous expletive: You fucking idiot, you wouldn't have fallen in love with me if I had told you. Deana, please come back. I'm even ready to get a gun licence to go fishing and hunting with some of your relatives who still do that sort of thing. *Bien sûr, pas de réponse.*

I use my sense of humour to pull myself out of this miserable state which doesn't have an ending. I think about the sunny day we went to the Hanlan's Point Beach. We took the ferry from the Jack Layton Terminal and then walked on the beautiful, hot sand.

"Remind you of Cuba?" I ask.

"Exactly. Mohammed. We're in the nude section. Mohammed, everyone's nude."

"I like it." I spread a large towel and invite her to sit down.

"Are you sure?"

"Deana. Take off your clothes."

"Okay I'll take off my stuff, but Mohammed I am not showing my twat to the entire gay community."

"Take those off. It's totally mixed here—*la pluralité des mondes*. Deana please show it, and stop being a vain back-to-the-land-spiritualist."

I'm feeling free in Toronto's liberated zone. Not a police officer in sight. The smell of weed is isotropic. Deana unbuttons her bright red blouse and takes it off in a way that has an effect on me. I look in the direction of some dense bushes near the beach. She takes off her bra. I rub Sun Protection Faction 30 on her back.

"Okay. I can feel the sun blazing my snatch." *Pyrolobus Fumarii* come to me from the depths of my vocabulary list. Would I have been better in Italian than maths? I wonder.

"This will save you from 96.7% of UVB rays, whereas an SPF of 50 means protection from about 98% of UVB rays. No sunscreens offer 100% protection from UVB rays. Sunlight will give you cancer."

"I don't want to get cancer so put more on me. And Mo' please put it on like a male prostitute." Lines like that reassure me that I've found a winner.

How can I bring her back? Can I dissolve this nebula inside me? Dr. H. Bar please shove the laser in my mouth, in my arsehole, up my dick, in my nose, but, somehow, save me.

As expected this little memory of her on the beach has made me be batty. It's night time and again, I'm walking endlessly in a park near my apartment. The Winter Hexagon consisting of Aldebaran, Capella, Castor, Pollux, Procyon, Sirius and Rigel hover over me and shoots down bullets of well-composed photons. I can't stop looking at Betelgeuse's uric colour.

High above the earth, I'm locked with Roy Orbison in a geostationary orbit over Lake Rosseau. He is playing his Gibson ES-335, in the key of F, the rest of his band members are floating away. His trademark dark glasses slip off his face and float away entering earth's upper atmosphere where they burn like silent sparklers. Roy's lips are moving but I can't hear the king of loneliness. I've walked all night. He had blue eyes. The early morning sunlight has blasted away all the *starry messengers*.

15. Canada Health Act

In the waiting area, I usually spend a few minutes giving my personal information to the kind and welcoming secretary. When my name is called I shift to the pre-exam room where I chat with the assistants. Across the years, I've had five resections, and I've gotten to know Musafareen who works in Urology Park. Thank Allah she hasn't burnt out yet. Nurses are severely over-worked; their salaries should be doubled right away. When she's prepping me, I turn the conversation to subjects that are going to distract me from the coming pain which is usually modest unless a laser is used. She is a minority of some kind or another.

Luckily, today, I bumped into her at the hospital cafeteria which has a high glassy open roof, and many chain restaurants that sell food so filled with sugar that eating anything on a regular basis would lead to a diabetic coma. I eat well at home and so, just before a cysto, I love eating a fried egg-in-a-bagel made by a chain. If Dr. H. Bar finds nothing, I'll have a Big Mac with large freedom fries, followed by a Smarties McFlurry. And a diet Root Beer.

Musafareen walks by me.

"Will you join me for coffee?" I ask her. With a gentle familiarity she sits across from me, but one seat over. I understand the rules.

"You have an appointment today?"

"Four times a year."

"Might seem like a lot but it's required," she says.

"Super uncomfortable."

"Yes, it is uncomfortable, but look, you're in great health. We do our best."

"I appreciate your help." All that metal, so frequently going into me, is turning me into Conscious Artificial Intelligence.

The remaining conversation touches on non-hospital issues; the failed Islamic state she left, the new life in Toronto, the greatness of the Canada Health Act. I can sense that work is calling her, and she leaves. In about half an hour, I'll meet her at UP where I'll read one of Deana's books on astronomy.

The lunch-time crowd thins. I leave for my cysto. I sit in the waiting room. My name is called out. I put on my blue gown. Musafareen helps me to lie down on the operating bed.

Dr. H. Bar walks into the examination room, "Mohammed, how are you?"

"Dr. Bar, I'm doing well. You'll find nothing at all today."

"I hope you're right," she says.

She doesn't have time for a small talk; she concentrates on her job. A million other bladders are waiting for her. I feel relaxed and steady. It's show time, but suddenly, I've gone nuts inside. Again. Oh, this is not a laser fulguration. Or is it? I've had so many that I forget what she's going to do this time. I'm here for a laser but didn't she laser me a few months back? A routine laser or a routine cysto—which for fuck's sake? Life becomes visits to the hospital.

I've lost my marbles. And, I am feeling sorry for myself. Or— wishful thinking—is this simply a surveillance of my low-grade bladder cancer after the Mitomycin cycle? I look upward to the monitor as though it were a church window. Musafareen hands her the 22-French flexible scope with a large *True Field of View*. Soon, the metal will travel the short-duration voyage to my bladder. The angel Musafareen is right beside me. Dr. Bar places herself between my spread legs. I'm reminded of a past operation when the cord unplugged, but that was another necessary cysto-daydream.

I feel my surgeon's masterful fingers on the head of my penis. I hear the usual: She's going in. I am going fucking nuts. Yes, Mohammed she's going in. It'll all be over soon. Mohammed, don't shit your pants. The monitor above my head shows a blur of water. I feel a slight pinch as she gently advances the camera in the direction of my pink piggy-bank bladder. She notices my pain, and confidently withdraws the snake, then she increases the water flow and re-enters. Now it doesn't hurt at all. She senses my discomfort when the steel tip advances up my urethra and slowly proceeds toward the bladder walls. Azaadi and Eddy could have done this on the island with sweet grass.

I'm thinking about my nurse carrying, in an upright uncovered jar, a cold liquid. She's run all the way from a desert war zone. Days of carrying that cold liquid from Addis Ababa to Toronto. Blessedly, she pours the entire bucket down my dick. The shadowless overhead light causes a crucifix on her neck to shine. A minority in the Islamic country she left, or a marriage with a Christian? Who cares, we're in Canada. No need to over-scrutinize.

The camera is an instrument I've been intimately familiar with all my artistic life. A version of it is now inside me. I feel the pinch at the urinary s-curve, the tunnel of my flesh opens up in a high gothic arc which I convert in my mind to the inside of Chartres Cathedral which is as large as another kind of cathedral: Europe's and the world's collective underground cathedral: *Conseil Européen pour la Recherche Nucléaire* (CERN). I am lighting votive candles illuminating the walls of the Cathedral of Chartres for all the suffering Saints who felt pain: St. Sebastian full of arrows, St. André spread out on his cross, large magnets over his hands and feet secure him to a metal cross.

I voyage from the church near my house, Our Lady of the Assumption on Bathurst Avenue to a veined map of the most beautiful cathedral in Christendom, my very own *Cathédrale Notre-Dame de Chartres* (CNDDC). The daydream holds off the mild pain.

"Please take a deep breath; this should not last long."

Like a pilot landing at YYZ during a fog, she's switched off auto pilot. She lands her instrument onto my fleshy runway outside the massive cathedral, buskers playing accordions for change outside. This easy landing has taken Helena twenty years of training. We're both camera users: I've mastered this machine which outlines truth over opinion and fantasy. I'm losing it—pain. Every three months. The laser is still in surveillance red mode.

In the invisible currents of saline solution the cancer undulates innocently—like flexible white stalactites hanging from my bladder walls. We can't see any cancer bits. What great news, but wait, there is always something. Where are you hiding? She'll find the fluttering papillary carcinoma.

The Roman Constant helps me to deflect the incidental pain. I'm now in my bladder, with my surgeon walking side by side. Squelch, squelch, her bare feet, no rubber boots. We hear Shostakovich's *Waltz 2*, which, after a few bars, climbs up my bladder walls mixing with the swirling water and bubbles. *Waltz 2* stops. Silence. That's good. I love silence. She's wearing green scrubs. I'm wearing a blue gown, my feet are treading on the cathedral floor, which is my bladder. A squelch sound made by red Adidas running shoes behind me with every bar of Shostakovich's delicious conjecture—this must be my guardian angel, Musafareen. I turn around, she's not there.

Now more music: Bach's *Mass in B minor* at the same time as *Waltz 2*. Both are playing at the same time, at the same volume. The sound of a cello flutters in the swirl of the clear fluid that she keeps gently pumping into the vaulting roof of Chartres. Then more dead silence. Now I hear the Soviet-era composer's 11th symphony playing at the same time as Bach—what noise. My head is bursting. All this music at the same time is making my equanimity a thing of the past. She makes the laser change colours from ecclesiastic candle orange to red to white. This colour change causes physical changes in the fucking new cancer bits. The trained heathen snake spits more calibrated photons which *dusts* all the new bits of growth. A cloud of debris obediently spirals downward before being sucked out of my bladder. Another zap. Ouch. Helena has *dusted* all the stalactites and stalagmites—all blown to high heaven. This saves me. Modern physics saves. The music stops. Silence and observation follow.

Who will see the next butterfly first? Helena or me? It's a game we play. A whitish butterfly carcinoma fluttering in the wind off the Atlantic a few kilometres south-west of Paris. But, hello, you're in Toronto, in a hospital, not Paris. Finding a new butterfly is probabilistic in nature, and dictated by a few random searches. My surgeon, and my friend the camera follow a dark blue vein in the shape of flying buttresses. She sees nothing more. She is not overawed: Thank Our Lady of the Angels of Chartres that she didn't see a great haul of variegated carcinoma. Thank the French. Thank the French for 1789. After a blood bath the French produced the best healthcare in the world. Otherwise, a priest wearing a cowl with filthy hands would be operating on me. Then on the way down the buttress, she hovers. Hovering is bad news. It's no longer painful. I'm used to it.

During a laser event a few months ago, she saw calcified bladder lesions—*zap*—they're now swirling like many Gabriels with broken wings. The fear of her hitting the laser button again encourages another thought experiment: This one takes me to a pew in the church of my bladder. Dr. H. Bar is walking beside me; then we sit down together, doctor, patient, in the holy sea of cancer. It feels nice to be inside my warm bladder with Dr. H. Bar. We're surrounded in fluid. Divinely, the question of breathing in saline does not arise. Trapped bubbles magnify something. Dr. Bar looks upwards along my bladder walls. Sitting on the pew together I say: "Is that dark reddish area a 2mm papillary urothelial neo-something? Is it malignant or as innocent as a daydream?"

"We just love it when patients detail their illness."

"I have to stay informed about my condition." Dr. Bar, please I wonder if you have any *Bedrooms of the Nation* or *Snow Blind Treaty*? Maybe we can smoke up in here? I've heard that blowing smoke on the bladder can fix it. With a tender glance, she ignores my question. No one listens to me. My friends tell their children: Don't listen to Mohammed.

"These are low-grade tumours. We deal with them by TURBT."

"What is a TURBT?" I ask her in the circulating water. Occasionally, we capture air bubbles with our mouths. The organist at Chartres walks past the organ; he doesn't sit down to play. The great Rose Window floats into view. *A TURBT is a procedure in which bladder tumors can be Transubstantiated into hosts.*

Dr. H. Bar sighs and recites the medical history. "Your medical report indicates that you had low-grade lesions in the anterior, as well as lateral walls; there were three lesions in total at that time. And you underwent repeat resections since; all showed an episode of gross hematuria." We're having this conversation in the echoing silence of my bladder. Dr. H. Bar, how do you know that *you* don't have bladder cancer? … I've zero episodes of gross hematuria … But Dr. Bar … Bar, you can't be sure … what are you saying? … why don't we examine your bladder while we're here? Do you think you'll find a solution to bladder cancer? I mean if all of the butterflies are controlled at the smallest sub-sub-subz atomic levels, at $2 \times 10^{(-10)}$ cm, why do we look at the surface of diseases and not at the korma subz level? Aren't I right? I must keep up this *distraction*. Did Benzophenone cause all this? I see Benzo Phlomenia magnetized to a cross.

When will my bladder have zero cancer? Up Quark, Down Quark. I am a dork who ate edible marijuana chocolate last night to make this hospital visit easier—it makes me see a homosexual muon—a fundamental subatomic particle—fighting a sex-changed Higgs boson.

Dimitri, without the interference of other music, is back. It's the youth orchestra from Arkhangelsk playing the ending of Shostakovich's best symphony: the 11th. A flute rising out of the smaller storm of strings bound together playing triads in C followed by thudding kettle drums followed by arching French Horns setting the stage for a worker's march. Holy Stradivari: We are hearing the clanging church bells and steel bars at the same time as the rippling Soviet field of orchestral strings. How can we examine my bladder when we're in yours, examining yours? I don't see why not. The camera is already here, so why don't you look and see if you have anything growing in yours? Dr. H. Bar is not offended.

A passacaglia increases in volume; all the double basses slide down, up or across to a major seventh and then move up, I don't know anything about music. On the pew, she turns towards me spreading her legs. She expertly inserts the camera's luminary head up her own urethra. The music reaches a crescendo. I sit on the oak pew, gawking at my surgeon's legs. Now we are both examining the walls of *her* bladder, which is, mercifully, free of butterflies.

Outside, looking at the monitor, Musafareen notices images of Dr. Bar's bladder replacing mine. Surgeons from a previous daydream, Claudio and Snakeopolis Pitosis, enter the fantasy and leave. Monarchs fill the operating room. Deana if I'd told you about my cysto experiences you would never have considered having me as a boyfriend. Did you want a boyfriend with a Uranium dick?

Cystoscopy during the December solstice: the number 7 bus in darkness. Cystoscopy at the March Equinox is the best because I've noticed that I have fewer papillary hoods beating me. Must be the French spring wind coming over Normandy causing the reduction in what she sees and zaps. The June solstice means even fewer butterflies; that's when I'm in front of the snake, wearing shorts and sandals, easier to get changed into the blue cassock for another examination.

The September equinox sees me buying new long johns in preparation for the winter solstices. Three visits a year for 10 years means at least 30 cytologies. I am going into my eighth decade with a bladder for all seasons.

Were I now living in the country I came from, I'd be dead. There, they don't tax the feudally better-off to protect the public from illness. Some of my closest friends with dark complexions want to privatize health care. They want to bring deep class inequality into Canada, just like back in the homeland. Secretly, they vote for hard right Canadian politicians but publicly say they vote for liberals. Mohammed didn't pay his fair share of taxes, so fuck him. That'll teach him.

As the leaves turn red and yellow, I continued with the BCG, that immunotherapy drug used to treat some non-invasive bladder cancer, three installations of 50 mg—but this is just what is called "maintenance". Before maintenance, I had six treatments spread across six glorious fall-coloured weeks. When talking with Dr. Bar in her office I saw her write *BCG failed* on a pink sheet in my file. Deana, pray for me.

"Okay, see you in three months. We'll see if the therapy is working."

"But what about the posterior aspect of the bladder on the left, which is papillary, low grade and noninvasive in appearance?"

Dr. Bar looks at me and blinks.

"Are you going to laser resect me again? What if you find two small bladder tumors in back wall of the bladder?" I continue: "Dr. Bar, I have a history of recurrent low-grade papillary urothelial carcinoma. What is governing their recurrence?" She sighs, but not impatiently. Particle physics and solutions for cancer are old hat; she knows that, I know that. I am just making chit-chat because I am a pure time-pass wallah.

I think she is saying, approximately, my prostate showed moderate trilobar hypertrophy. Today you were brought into the Cystoscopy Suite. You were prepped and draped. I inserted a flexible scope into your dick's head. You said ouch, I said stay calm, I'll save you. The anterior urethra appeared like a clean church. We surveyed the mucosa. We didn't see multiple small papillary recurrences. In the past, we saw, in the posterior bladder wall a low-grade urothelial carcinoma approximately 5000 kilometres in size. Mohammed, just kidding. It was 5mm. There were four other small superficial papillary-appearing growths on the bladder floor, near the trigone. These all measured 1-2 kilometres in size. The ureteric orifices looked uninvolved and had clear ureteric jets. The rest of the bladder appeared normal except for cancer vectors in which there are two quarks moving beside massless butterflies going in the direction of Uranus. The scope was then withdrawn, we took a urine sample for the piss museum.

Dimitri's *11th Symphony in G minor, Op 103* ends. The calming sound of gushing water increases, but paradoxically, this is causing me some pain. We need continuous bladder irrigation.

Gracefully, Dr. H. Bar pilots the scope out of my bladder. *Inshallah*, we'll land; *Inshallah*, the non-invasive tumours will become things in my past.

"Okay all good. I didn't see anything. Looks like the Mitomycin C with EMDA is working. See you in three months." More surveillance. The Ontario Health Insurance Plan does not pay for Mitomycin C with EMDA. I had to pay $2112. I live on a pension. I called OHIP twice. OHIP agents should have studied the French Revolution, and the precise role of the guillotine in social progress.

Sometimes, when Helena says she found nothing, I feel like crying, but I don't. The routine pain has made me brave. Azaadi, this will make you respect me.

Without nurses like Musafreen I'd be helpless. Nurses should get paid as much as university professors, certainly more than bullshit producing contemporary philosophers.

A few minutes later, I meet Dr. Bar in her large office for our post-examination chat. She'll have to return to my watery Chartres; she found something that needs resection, nothing serious. I prepare for resection number seven. My tiny boxing match with controllable cancer will continue. Not even Golden Mitomycin with EDMA can permanently stop the persistent small growths.

I'll create a few daydreams for future cystos. These will set the dramatic stage for Helena or one of her fellows—perhaps that kind fellow, Dr. Abdul Ansari Abdullah from Kabul who examined me when her case load was too busy. I say *Allah-o-Akbar* as my bladder tenderly moves through the verdant equinoxes to the blazing white solstices, year after year.

16. Muskoka mon amour

My phone buzzes. "Azaadi. How are you? Calling from Lake Rosseau?"

"Yeah, from Rosseau. Mo', I'm fine."

"How's Renée? Give her my best. How's Eddy?" I think of Renée's lovely voice.

"Everyone is fine. Mohammed, earlier I sent you a message by falcon. I didn't get a response, so that's why I am calling you. Mohammed, I'm inviting you to a party slash house-warming. It's at Eddy's house—near my place. He just finished his new cottage. He'd like you to come for the house-warming. We'll meet first."

I look out from my window, I see and hear robins and cardinals, no falcons.

"I'll be glad to be with you and Eddy again."

"Deana will be there. She'd like to say hello. She needed time."

"I'll catch the bus. Can you pick me up?"

"No problem, except you don't need to catch the bus. Eddy's in Toronto at an international rice growers convention. He's going to call to arrange a pick-up time. Wednesday okay? His new car is a *Lucid Air*."

Wednesday morning is time-stamped into my head. I wake up at 05:00; bag packed and excited about Eddy's late afternoon arrival. I take my blood pressure—it's slightly above normal—thankfully she's the only possible cause of it.

Eddy texts me from outside my place, I lock up my apartment and walk to his car.

"Mohammed, man. All's good with you? That was a load of puking we did, eh? The nutritionist in me was frowning. Azaadi thought our methods got twisted-up somehow, no doubt by our internet searches. Anyways, do you have another brand name for a weed company? Rice slash weed combo."

"I will by the time we hit the 400, promise."

"Can't wait to hear it."

"Eddy, is your sound system as good as Deana's?"

"You'll find out when you come up with a brand name."

We push through the Bathurst street late rush-hour traffic in silence. We don't drive past Daoud's house. Then, the release onto the Highway 400 and the North. "A Beatles song. *Things We Said Today*, okay with you."

He voices the request into the system, thankfully the system doesn't ask for a million confirmations of commands. Eddy starts bellowing the lyrics idiotically. We pass the Holland Marsh, then Barrie. John, Paul, George and Ringo carry us over the Severn onto the Shield and its majestic, red granite outcrops.

"*Sgt. Pepper's?*"

"No. Too Mod for me."

"Me too. Too modern, you're right. I like their earlier stuff. It's a week-day, so no cops on the road. Do you mind if I speed up? I mean like really floor it."

"Hey, I got your brand name: *High School* no make that *Higher Education*."

"Will sell big-time."

"Make any new friends at the rice conference? New friends from Wogland?"

"Wogland—what the fucks's that?"

"Make any connections from India?"

"Jesus, yes. Indians, I loved them. Their food stalls are good. Really, good. And they're so friendly but it's difficult to understand them. You don't sound like them—what happened to you?"

"They're from India. I'm from Pakistan. In Pakistan, we all sound like we're from the suburbs of London, especially right in Pakistan itself."

"Go figure, eh? I'll fly to Wogland to get rice seeds, then with some genetic intervention we'll mix Basmati and wild rice and get it to grow in three seasons right in Muskoka.

"I got your brand name for the Muskoka grown-brown rice: *Red Basmati.*"

"Very funny. Ha ha."

"Why don't you sponsor some rice workers from India to help you out? They know technique. Those small-acreage private farmers who've been run off their land by Big Agriculture corporations. I'm being serious. In a way, there'd be Indians Citizens again in Muskoka. I mean ones with Indian passports. In no time at all, they'd outnumber the Hollywooders. They'd get Californian accents."

"Mo', you think big. Gotta hand it to you. Great suggestion but not doable. Frankly, you're nuts. Fucking nuts. But. You always make me laugh. I'd become road kill if I did that. The white press would call it racketeering or slave labour. Imagine us *Injuns* exploiting Indians—a story with a twist. Passport Indians. Jesus. Mo', you're nuts."

"Could be the first case in world history where Canada's indigenous people are accused of exploiting Indian Citizens."

"Yes. Mo', you should do standup."

"I think I'm too shy."

"You could try a dry run at a Pow Wow. The labour racketeering bit will crack em up. For sure. But don't say a thing about cutting those grants to the chiefs, okay?"

We cross the Severn. I don't say anything nor does he. The ancient rock outcrops glide by. After a while I ask: "How did you get to know Azaadi?"

"Yeah, we're from the same community if that's what you mean. We lived on the same compound in Saudi Arabia—you could call it a reserve of sorts. I know that's what you're thinking inside anyway. We met Saudi progressives, and Saudi feminists, and some not so progressive. We had a laugh. I was a pilot. Bombardier A Global 7500. I'm licensed and up to date. Took them to Japan. I have a small plane at my cottage. Want a spin?"

"I'd love that. Who'd you fly for in Saudi?"

"The smaller families. Meanest mother-fuckers in the world. Worse than these Hollywood cottagers. At least the Hollywoods don't slap the shit out of their Filipinas maids. These super rich had gold threads sewn right in their clothing: How fucking nuts is that? I used to take Azaadi on regional flights around the Gulf. Trick is to stay out of Iranian air space. They have missiles that can make you history. Your bladder would be fixed along with you."

"You saw the really rich in the Kingdom?"

"Brother Mohammed: The word *rich* has no meaning. These oil guys have so much moola that it's kinda abstract, really. We flew them or their sons and daughters for short shopping trips to Dubai: Why do Saudis need fur coats? I piloted one trip so the man could fly to another nearby country to buy exactly one pack of cigarettes. One pack."

"Fur coats? Why? Canadian beavers?"

"No beavers. I think they used artificial fur. Kinda ethical if you ask me. Ethical Saudis. They need fur coats for the snow slopes in Dubai. Some were super kind, and deep thinkers. Indoor ski slopes. Cooled to -5C. Drugs and Natashas 8000 metres above the desert. Think of that. Fun to see a coke-loaded Arab trying to fly a jet—under supervision, of course. All this shit was an eye-opener for a bush pilot like me: Saudi Arabia's first Indigenous pilot."

Muskoka transforms into *Rub' al Khali*: The Canadian shield is covered with skyscraper hotel towns with palm trees in Baysville, falling coconuts in Bracebridge, mango groves around Gravenhurst and Dorset. His phone rings. He puts Azaadi on speaker.

"Eddy. Hello. When do you arrive?"

"We're about 20 minutes out. Permission to land."

"Permission to land? Eddy, are you crazy? You're not flying, are you? The lake is frozen over. Hello … Come in, Eddy, Where are you landing?"

"Azaadi buddy, relax. I was kidding. I'm driving. You're on speaker, Mohammed is right beside me. Don't say anything mean about him. Told him about our trips in the Middle East. By the way, Mo' wants another sauna and a better makeup job."

"Eddy, you're on speaker also. The house lights are off. Land blind."

We hear Renée. "Eddy and Mo', hello. We're looking forward to seeing you. Eddy, keep your hands on the steering wheel. Don't let the autopilot fool you."

"See you in a few." Eddy hangs up.

At Azaadi's, we don't get out immediately. From the car, we see Azaadi wearing a massive brown fur coat. Renée is wrapped in white fur. I don't let any value judgements sit in my mind in case he can read them. Hopefully, that connection has ended and another deeper friendship is forming. Telepathy can limit a friendship.

They follow us along a rural road until we arrive at a raised plateau on top of which stands Eddy's prefabricated palace. The minaret imported brick-by-brick from Saudi Arabia looks good with the Moorish window balconies. Later Eddy told me that the minaret were not imported brick by brick but were made brick-by-brick by ultra local construction workers; only a few were muslims. In the distance, on the horizon we see a band of pine trees silhouetted against the dark night sky. A wide stairway, obeying the rules of perspective, goes to the lake. Their car doors open like a gull alighting in a field.

"Don't tell me, same lake as Azaadi's?"

"Yep, eastern side where the Windermere once stood. Eddy's house does not have the modern floating in the air effect."

"I like the understated design of yours more."

"You think I went overboard on the Indian theme, don't you?"

We step into his house. Trance house-music thuds gently across the birch wood floor. Urban colonized fool that I am; I was expecting those ear-shattering drums and moose burgers, but Eddy had a Japanese spread. Tons of mixed folk standing round, eating with chop sticks, some dancing. Everyone from the planet Earth is here at Eddy's place in Muskoka. Some older people sit off to the side. At the back of his place, I see a parked single-engine float airplane. Azaadi approaches.

"So did you like my coat? It's genuine Algonquin Park black bear. Did you judge me? Just kidding. I can't do it anymore, don't worry. Thought I'd goose you with that question though. Telepathy is not too good for friendship. So good to see your face. How do you like Ed's place?—guy even sleeps with his twin-engine plane right beside him. Strange don't you think?"

"I noticed a single engine float plane." Azaadi gives me a long, tight hug.

I am impatient to see Deana. I look everywhere for her lips. Will things cohere and synchronize or synchronize and cohere?

I walk around and chat with various groups of people—all friendly. I eat smoked eel from the wall-to-wall Sushi selections. I speak with someone named Chan.

"So how'd you end up here?"

"We're all friends—from U of T."

Dancing while he talks, he drifts away to join a woman who is eating a Silken tofu dessert. "Some are from Science Engineering and others are friends of Deana's. Eddy is our general uncle. Talk later. Got to dance."

A few tall women with large hands, perhaps Renée's friends, have integrated into the line dance which nicely exposes their dance moves as something from a previous era. A VJ named *VJ Iron Heron* projects clips from old racist Hollywood films organized by decades. Champagne flows like the Assiniboine. Looks like Indigenous People took off into the future using good old-fashioned capitalism to get to a point in their lives where there weren't any irresolvable land disputes, to live happily with white settler elites and Pakistani settlers. Money, like new windshield wipers, squeegeed away some if not all land disputes. But I think about all of the Indigenous People who don't have a lot of money or own a lot of land, like the locals in Muskoka who could no longer afford to pay land taxes.

I sit down and start chatting with an older man who tells me about his life as a steel worker in New York. He spent most of his youth working high above the city. He moved from Kahnawake to work on the Empire State and Chrysler buildings.

"Many industrial accidents?" I ask. I think he must be ancient with deep rivers crossing his face.

"I saw a photograph with a bunch of people sitting out on a steel beam having lunch. I'd be scared shitless to be out on that beam."

"We weren't scared. Good money in the work. Nice apartments in Brooklyn. I bought a convertible Chevy Impala, used to drive it back home on the weekends."

Azaadi introduces me to his friends. He tells one Quechua speaker that I speak a South Asian form of Quechua. Through thick bifocals, the elder speaks Quechua in my direction. I look at Azaadi, my hands conversationally turning upward, "What should I do? I am not sure he understands Urdu. I only speak it when I'm pretending to be self-othering."

"Don't worry. Here's Aiyana. She's our Urdu-Quechua translator."

I look at Aiyana who is dressed in a shiny black suit. She has smaller hands, and obviously understands Azaadi's sense of fun. She lets out a mild laugh and smiles. The elder asks me something in Quechua; Aiyana, smiling, translates. He's convinced I understand him fully. I respond in my kitchen Urdu: the kind that I use when ordering food in a Pakistani restaurant to impress white friends. It appears we are talking about how small the world has become. In comes Quechua out goes Urdu. Aiyana translates my Urdu into Quechua. He laughs and asks me another question via Aiyana. I answer back in Urdu. He laughs as soon as Aiyana has finished translating. Azaadi is amused by the fact that everyone knows that no one understands each other. Yet we had a meaningful exchange. Funny how language works.

Deana has walked into our conversation. A change in air pressure.

"Dad, why pull a stunt like that on poor Mohammed? He knows enough Urdu to order a Shami Kebab with allo gobi and roti in a restaurant run by white locals in Huntsville. At least he knows more Urdu than you know Quechua."

Deana is looking right into my eyes. A universe of cosmic pluralism had opened. I thank Allah and the bear spirits.

"Mohammed is doing research," Azaadi says. "Isn't that right Mohammed?"

"Azaadi, you're right. I'll figure out how to put it in the new book. I'll thank you in the acknowledgements."

Azaadi politely slides up to us and walks into the party.

Deana has moved closer to me. She has taken off her gloves and is touching my hand. I think about washing her feet in the shower. "Mohammed. I needed time. That's all. I've missed you like a telescope misses The Milky Way."

It's a moonless, dark sky. The Muskoka air, which all immigrants from polluted China love, is transparent. The stars hover above us in 3D. The winter air flows onto a large, enclosed balcony with pillars dividing and branching at the top like a Mogul palace, perhaps with confused Doric, Ionic or Corinthian references. Above us the Belt of Orion and his sword surges in our faces. My heart is going like mad. I look up to see Messier 42—the very heart of Orion's sword. She's pushed her warm body against me.

Her lips have become real, not just detached objects in my memory. As soon as we kiss, someone sets off fireworks which are ultra-luminous. I turn around and look out. Eddy is bending down with a cigarette lighter. A hissing *Missile* firework rises toward red super giant Betelgeuse, and explodes in front of the constellation, creating bright particles that fall down in arcs. This is followed by a *Dahlia*—a shell that mimics an exploding starfish. I'm smelling fruit-flavoured explosives in the fireworks burning in front of the Rigel, only 863 light years away. And those stars are also exploding; they're burning hydrogen into helium. The open clusters of young white hot stars are sending us the very elements needed to make these romantic, sentient firecrackers.

"Mohammed, this next one is a *Tourbillion*. Watch the variation of RGB light." The point of light of the firework reaches its maximum height and explodes emptying its sparkling intestines over Muskoka.

"When I felt your hand and we kissed these fireworks launched. What timing." She turns around to wave at Eddy.

"I told Eddy to light the fireworks when I kiss you. Dad had the fireworks delivered from Bompas & Parr." She's laughing and holding me tight.

"You set up this party?"

"Mohammed, how are you?" Momentarily unmoored, I respond: "They found nothing in three sequential bladder examinations. Those few hours on the island combined with white-man's medicine worked. *Inshallah*, Dr. H. Bar will find nothing in the near future. Your fireworks were nearly a corporate endeavour. Must have cost tons."

I put my hand inside her coat and lift up her sweater and touch her warm back. The entire party is outside watching the fireworks.

In a few minutes, we return to the human warmth of the ballroom and see a long row of twenty-something foreign students do another mock line-dance set to danceable European Trance House music. The dancers work in unison, then break out into dance solos. The older people clap and sway to the electronic music. Ageless social harmony. The dancers, some from Wuhan, intermix with other settlers from New Delhi, Assam, Dublin, London, Paris and from various very small South American communities and some locals Muskokans. A skilled dancer breaks into a solo dance; the other dancers surround her. She then quickly pirouettes into the line, *wining and jamming* to the perfect thud thud. "You set this up too?"

"Not the line dance. That just happened on its own. Look—some of my friends are here. We'll meet them in a while."

In the near distance, Azaadi and Renée are talking with animation. They look toward Deana and me and lift their glasses of bubbly, then meander over to chat with us. Renée reaches into her pocket, pulls out her phone and gives it to Azaadi. He displays the screen first to his daughter and then to me: "Two tickets for you and Deana to go to San Pedro, Chile, to see the night sky, 4000 metres up. It's an all-inclusive, you can take a stargazing tour if you want. You'll like it. You can't say no."

"Dad. Renée. Thank you. Thank you. Mohammed can go," Deana says.

"Thank you Azaadi and Renée. I'm not sure what to do. I've never been that far south or that high."

"Leaving day after tomorrow. Eight days. You'll have a great time. And I got you two a nice hotel and you can have a mud bath nearby. Mud at 4000 metres."

"Mohammed, please say yes."

"Do we have time to go to my place so I can pack?"

The Air Canada jet takes us to Santiago where we wait for ages before boarding our flight to San Pedro. We fly over the desert and, as soon as we step into San Pedro de Atacama, the altitude hits me.

I gulp for air, I get a day-long headache. The town is in the arid high plateau in the Andes mountains of northeastern Chile. The inescapable fact is that this is our honeymoon, but without the moon. Azaadi selected moonless nights for better seeing.

I'm short of breath. I can see and count the red corpuscles in front of my eyes. I can stand still, that's no problem, but I have trouble sleeping. I can't think of going near her *Canes Venatici*, so we just hold each other. We drive some distance to have a morning mud bath followed by a lunch of pork ribs cooked in an "horno de barro"—an oven with adobe walls.

The sunlight up here hits us much much harder than at lower altitudes. It almost burns. The days are cloudless, and I've never seen such a dark night sky in my life. It's much better than going to a European art museum. At a telescope site, she rents a large solar scope with a H-alpha filter. We see a deep red sometimes orange sun, and another Albania prominence, hunting for carbon-based life, floats away into the black sky. We discover little black dots on the sun's surface. She tells me about native constellations with difficult-to-pronounce names.

She's established a daily routine: DSOs and planets at night, then local exploration. One afternoon she organizes a trip to the Valle de la Luna and Los Flamencos National Reserve where there are two lakes: *Miscanti* and *Miñiques*—about an hour's drive from San Pedro. We see the sky turn pink with Los Flamencos. It is *Terra incognita* for me. The corpuscles vanish from my eyes and now, given where we are, I've risen madly in love with her.

One day after a lunch of fish soaked in lemon, I light a local version of *Snow Blind Treaty*, then finally, after days of adjustment, we make love post-mud, and literally seconds after, we head out. Sometimes, she's packed too many events into our schedule.

From Santiago, the Air Canada jet climbs up through all the fascist airspaces to YYZ. A new phase of my life starts with Deana at the centre. Months flow into years, then Deana asks me to move into her beautiful apartment.

"I can't move in with you. I want and need my independence. And you leave your hair in the sink."

"Mo', dear. I've stopped listening to you. You'll get to drive my Tesla anytime. Move in."

I continue living in my apartment near Bathurst and Eglinton. I work on a short novel on Mondays, Tuesdays and Wednesdays. From Wednesday evening to Monday morning I stay with her. On Mondays I return to my place. Her car doesn't have a key. It unlocks when I am within a metre of its door as if it smells me. Maybe it reads my mind like Azaadi. She's synchronized my emission nebula with the Tesla's door lock, proving without the shadow of a doubt that we have a love that will never die.

Acknowledgements

I thank the following people for commenting on the manuscript: Benjamin Shaer, Claudio Gaudio, Edwin Gailits, Hein Marais, Leslie de Freitas, Michael Ryan, Ricardo Sternberg, Richard Sanders, Ron Booth and Sean Kane.

About the Author

Currently residing in Toronto after living in Montreal for three decades, **Julian Samuel** is a writer, and painter. Publications include novels: *Passage to Lahore*, and *Radius Islamicus*. He has directed many documentaries including: *The Raft of the Medusa: Five voices on colonies, nations and histories, Into the European Mirror, City of the Dead and the World Exhibitions, Save and Burn* and *Atheism*. His articles and essays have appeared in *Canadian Literature* and *Fuse, Race and Class, The Montreal Gazette, Le Devoir, La Presse, Counterpunch, Books in Canada* and *Montreal Serai. Muskoka* is his third novel. For more information on past and recent work see his website: www.julianjsamuel.com

Printed by Imprimerie Gauvin
Gatineau, Québec